HER RELUCTANT BOSS

ESCAPE TO SUN VALLEY

SARAH GAY

LITERARY EVOLUTION

ALSO BY SARAH GAY

All books in the
Grant Brothers Billionaire Boss Romance
Series:

Her Reluctant Boss: Book 1
sarahgay.com/her-reluctant-boss

The Billionaire Patriot: Book 2
sarahgay.com/the-billionaire-patriot

The Billionaire Smokejumper: Book 3
sarahgay.com/the-billionaire-smokejumper

The Billionaire Champion: Book 4
sarahgay.com/the-billionaire-champion

The Billionaire Hockey Star: Book 5
sarahgay.com/the-billionaire-hockey-star

Once Upon a Midnight Kiss: Book 6
sarahgay.com/once-upon-a-midnight-kiss

The Billionaire Fake Fiancé: Book 7
sarahgay.com/the-billionaire-fake-fiance

The Last Billionaire: Book 8
sarahgay.com/the-last-billionaire

NEWSLETTER—FREE BOOK, GIVEAWAY, AND SPECIAL OFFERS

To receive a free copy of Sarah Gay's best-selling book, Her Guardian Boss Fake Fiancé, simply join her mailing list on her website SarahGay.com.

By signing up, you'll get a first look at new releases, special offers, and learn how to register for giveaways.

Enjoy your FREE book today!

CHAPTER ONE

*S*imon sat on the piano stool and closed his eyes, allowing his mind to float back in time to when his fingers danced across the slick ivory keys in the expensive café in Paris. He smiled at how he'd earned a free meal and made a few extra bucks that one night three years ago when he'd sat down at the vacant piano stool of the crowded restaurant on a dare and played a unique rendition of "C'est Si Bon." The aroma of roasted onions and truffles sizzling in butter wafted through the Mandolin restaurant, bringing his memories of France to the forefront of his mind; he could almost taste the thick Parisian air, silty with baguette flour.

"How's my star pupil?" boomed a familiar voice.

Simon's eyes popped open and he jumped from the piano stool to hug his old piano instructor, Roy. Roy was only a few years older than Simon, but he'd been a master at the piano before he'd lost all his baby teeth. Simon could hardly fit his arms around the guy; Roy's girth had increased over the past five years. "How's my favorite hunter?" Simon asked. Roy was an excellent shot as well as an excellent musician.

"The prodigal son has returned." Roy chuckled as he

returned Simon's hug. "I'm guessing you're the guy the job coach from Workforce Services should talk to when he comes in. He wanted to stop by and discuss the employees he's sent us with special needs."

"When will he be here?"

"I think he said he'll be coming in before we open. What are *you* doing here tonight?"

"We're low on bussers. I promised my great-grandpa I'd come in and help out."

"Good to have you *back*," Roy said, giving Simon a hearty smack on the back.

"It's good to be—" Simon lost his train of thought when the most beautiful woman he'd ever seen sauntered into the room. His eyes widened as her long legs carried her across the room with unforgiving confidence, but she didn't walk to impress; she couldn't have known that she had an audience. Her huge green eyes smiled at Roy but didn't make their way to Simon. Simon blinked a few times while his gaze followed her swift steps across the room until she ultimately disappeared into the kitchen.

Roy patted Simon on the shoulder. "Sometimes it takes coming home to realize what you've been missing."

Simon blew out a breath he hadn't realized he'd been holding. "I'd say. Who is she?"

"*She's* too good for you. Don't even think about her," said Roy.

Simon pulled at his beard. That sounded like a challenge. "We'll see about that."

Roy laughed. "Have you looked in the mirror lately? With your shaggy hair and unkempt beard, you look like you're the long-lost Sasquatch who happened to stumble out of the woods and into this fine gastronomic establishment for a snack."

"By the end of the night," Simon said with a cunning smile, "she'll be asking me for *my* phone number."

Roy held out his hand. "Fifty bucks?"

"You're on," said Simon, giving Roy's hand a firm shake.

~

*H*annah Fields swayed to the live piano music as she walked across the Mandolin restaurant. She'd never been to France, but when she was in the restaurant, with its bright mustard walls decorated with Impressionist-styled paintings in thick gold frames, she could've sworn she was there. Roy played French piano music during the three hours the five-star French restaurant was open in the evenings, adding to the ambiance—until the end of the night, when he played Hannah's favorite blues compilation. He knew she liked the more upbeat blues, like "When You're Smiling..." She didn't mind the romantic Parisian café music, but she loved ending her shift to the deep silky sounds of the old-town blues.

She leaned across the table of the empty booth and blew out a dying candle. Casting a quick glance back at her last customers, who were sitting at the farthest table across the room, she discreetly stretched out her sore legs by pushing up off the table as she stood back up. The Mandolin restaurant had been busy tonight, but that wasn't why her legs ached; she'd skied hard the last few days to get in as much fresh air and spring sunshine as possible before the resorts closed for the season. The snow had been slushy and thick, so it had been like trying to ski across the sticky side of duct tape, but it was well worth the effort—as was the subsequent pain it left her in. She loved her mountains; she'd been away from them for far too long. She was finally home to stay—for good.

With the end of ski season came the end of busy shifts at the Mandolin. Hopefully, she'd get the job tomorrow. She needed the money. Her interview with the Law Offices of Grant and Grant could be her opportunity to settle down in the valley where she'd been raised. She'd finally be able to live like she had as a kid before her parents' divorce—before all the comforts of wealth had disappeared. She was tired of being poor in a town where the rich and famous flocked in to ski in the winter, then returned in the summer to golf, hike, and ride horses. And the wealthy residents were only getting richer; there was a millionaire for every poor kid and a billionaire for every widow. Hannah laughed to herself while she wiped down the next table; the local joke on the street was that every local widow sought out her own personal billionaire to wed.

While Hannah spritzed the table with antibacterial spray, then wiped it down with the damp white cloth, she wondered where the busser had gone. He'd followed her around all evening, clearing her tables. She wanted to tip him out and thank him for his hard work.

The managers at the Mandolin had big hearts. They typically employed older individuals with special needs to bus the tables, or kids in high school who needed discipline. She wondered if the busser had special needs. She'd seen him talking to the job coach from Workforce Services who'd come in earlier to check on his placements, but the busser didn't appear to be mentally slow. He wasn't physically slow, either; he'd cleaned Hannah's tables the moment her customers stood to leave. He had a rough appearance, like he'd lived on the streets for a time, but there were moments that evening while she rushed from table to table when she'd caught him staring at her. His eyes were a warm honey brown and surprisingly alert; they didn't have the dazed look she'd seen on the faces of people who lived on the streets.

But to be working as a busboy at his age? He must have come from hard circumstances or had a mental disability.

At least he was more interesting than the young brats who sometimes bussed for her. *Sometimes bussed for me?* She laughed at herself. She'd only been home for a few weeks since she'd passed the bar. The owners of the Mandolin were kind to always hire her when she was in town. The kids who came to bus tables were millionaire brats with insanely bad attitudes and phone addictions. The only time she could remember rich kids bussing tables and doing a decent job at it was when the Grant brothers took their turns in high school for a year or two before they left for college.

She'd been in the same grade as one of the Grant brothers. She searched her mind for his name, then snapped her fingers: Levi. When she and Levi were young, they'd been friends. They'd gone to the same private school together, along with Levi's older brother and five younger brothers. She'd never been able to keep them straight; they were all so close in age and appearance.

After Hannah's parents had gotten divorced when she was in high school, her father had taken off with his mistress and every penny of her parents' savings; he'd left them and their hefty house payment behind. Hannah's mom went back to work, and Hannah started attending public schools. She didn't see Levi again until they worked together at the Mandolin their senior year of high school, but he hadn't recognized her. She was a hostess and he was a busser. He'd never said one word to her that entire year they worked together. He hadn't been rude to her; he simply kept his distance. She chalked it up to him not knowing who she was or that she even existed.

Their lives had been set on different trajectories. He'd been sent to an Ivy League institution back east. She'd attended a community college, gone on to graduate with a

BA in English from the University of Idaho, then gotten into their law school. And here she was, finally back in her favorite place and ready to work, but employment was limited. If she wanted to stay in the beautiful little hamlet of Sun Valley and Ketchum, she needed a decent-paying job to cover the high cost of living.

She didn't mind not being rich. In fact, she wanted nothing to do with the pomp and glam that flew in on their sleek corporate jets and posh helicopters. She'd had plenty of suggestive offers over the past few weeks from both Hollywood and Wall Street. It hadn't been difficult to turn them down; she wanted to make it on her own terms. She wouldn't make the same mistake her mother had, marrying a wealthy man with wandering eyes who kept a sleazy attorney in his back pocket. She'd be the attorney to knock the sleaze back to where he came from. She planned on marrying a family man, not a man who stopped into her little town on his journey to fortune and fame. Her mind was set on a settler, not a wanderer.

"Excuse me. Can I help you?" the tall, hairy busser said as he reached across the table and picked up the candle and salt and pepper shakers. For a bushy nomad, he sure smelled good.

"Yeah. Thanks," she said with a tender smile. "You did a great job tonight. Don't leave before I can tip you out, okay?"

His mouth opened into a toothy grin, displaying straight white teeth. Perfect teeth weren't what she was expecting from his gruff appearance. She thought he'd have at least one missing tooth. "I'm okay," he said with an adorable blink of his caramel eyes. He didn't seem slow, but by the kind way in which he stared into her eyes, he could be somewhere on the spectrum.

"Look, you saved me tonight. After I get payment from this last table, meet me at the piano."

He nodded and walked away, but not before he caught the glimmer of amusement that lit his eyes. She couldn't imagine why, other than that he simply had a happy, kind demeanor, as did most people she'd known with mental disabilities.

The men at the last occupied table in the restaurant didn't look like they were anywhere near ready to leave with how they were still joking around. She'd dropped their check off to them twenty minutes earlier, and they still hadn't touched it. She'd never had to kick customers out before, but perhaps she could hurry them along.

She stepped up to the table and spoke loudly. "How are we doing over here? Can I get you some more water and take that check for you?"

The middle-aged men looked up at her simultaneously and their laughter cut short. The man closest to her with a thick mustache nodded. "Could you bring us another ..." He held up his glass.

She bowed slightly. "I apologize, but the bar is closed for the evening."

The man slammed his glass back down onto the table. Luckily, the owners had invested in high-quality glassware, saving the man's hand from injury. "I have a better idea, Hannah," the man said, staring at her name tag before his eyes wandered to her chest. "Come with me and I'll take you to a place where the bar is still open, and I'll buy you a drink."

She tried to shield the anger from her voice. "That is kind of you, but I'll be closing up tonight. If we could get your check taken care of, our hosts will help you get to your next destination safely."

"The only destination I want to get is right here," the man said, placing his large hand on her bottom.

Before Hannah had a chance to smack away his hot hand, the hairy busboy grabbed him by his shoulder and threw him to the ground. The man stumbled to his feet and took a

7

swing at the busser, connecting with his cheekbone, then reached for his throat. The busser responded with a punch to the man's jaw. The man's eyes rolled back in his head and he slumped to the floor.

The middle-aged man's friends jumped from their seats and started yelling until Roy stepped between them with a growl. "We're leaving!" one of them shouted. They quickly grabbed their bloody friend, who had woken with a moan, and plowed out of the restaurant.

"What were you thinking!" Hannah shouted at the busser. "You could've gotten hurt."

He looked at her with an expression of shock.

Hannah blew out a long, slow breath. She hadn't meant to hurt his feelings. She grabbed his hand, still formed into a fist, and examined it for injury. "But thanks." She motioned with her head to a booth. "Come sit down and let me look at you in a better light." She glanced at Roy, who was walking back into the room after escorting the scum out of the restaurant. "Roy, could you get us some ice, please?"

Roy's face hardened when he looked at the busser.

"Roy, please," Hannah insisted. Why would Roy be upset with the sweet busser?

"Okay," Roy muttered as he pushed open the door to the kitchen.

Hannah scooted in next to the busboy on the bench and turned to face him. She carefully pushed his hair away from his face to get a good look at his cheek. The flesh under his eye had already started to darken. "Looks like you got yourself a shiner."

"It was worth it," he said, staring into her eyes.

A zing of excitement shot through her center. She turned her eyes down momentarily to avert his gaze. When she looked back up, he was still staring at her intently. "No, it wasn't," she argued.

"Yes. It was," he said with a smile.

She shook her head, trying not to smile back at him. "Now you're just being difficult."

Roy handed Hannah a small bag of crushed ice. "Here you are," he said with a light chuckle. "Wouldn't want to spend too much time with a difficult man. I'll be at the piano if you need me." He nodded to the busser, then walked away.

Hannah frowned. Roy had never stuck around to play the piano after all the customers had left. "Hmm, Roy's acting odd, but he's the sweetest guy. And how he plays the piano …" She sighed. "It makes me smile."

The busser lifted his brows with apparent interest. "You like it when a man plays the piano for you?"

As if on cue, Roy began playing a blues song she'd never heard him play before, "Ain't No Sunshine."

Hannah tipped her head to the side in thought. "That's an unusually sad song for Roy to play," She applied the ice lightly to the busser's cheek. "How does that feel?"

"Amazing," he said with a blink of his eyes. "I'm sorry about those creeps."

She shook her head in anger. "Some people think they can do anything because they have money. It makes me sick. I'd date a rich man just as soon as I'd swim in crocodile-infested waters."

The busser coughed. "You can also swim with gentle manatees in Florida, the same place you find crocodiles. What's sick is how those old guys thought they could touch you."

She sighed out her agreement. "How old are you?"

"Twenty-nine."

"Really?" she asked with surprise. "You're only two years older than me."

He gave her hand a light squeeze and smiled, causing her heart to flutter. Only then did she realize she'd been holding one of his hands the entire time they'd sat together on the bench; it felt so natural. He raised his free hand and dragged his fingertips down her chin. "Will you go out with me?"

She wanted to say yes, but her internal compass stopped her. *What am I doing to this sweet guy who isn't all mentally there?* He was cute, but they didn't have a future together, and she tried not to lead any guy on, especially one so tender. "No." She released his hand, scooted off the bench, and stood. "It's not a good idea."

He scratched at his beard as he stood. "Is it because I'm a busser?"

She wrinkled her nose. "Sort of." She didn't want to hurt his feelings any more than she had to.

"I see." With a disappointed sigh, he turned to walk away.

She held up a finger. "Wait. I haven't tipped you out yet."

He pulled his wallet out of his pocket, silently held up a fifty-dollar bill, and placed it in Roy's glass jar next to the piano. "Tip Roy. He's earned it tonight."

Roy nodded, but he didn't smile his appreciation to the busser like he normally did after he'd received a healthy tip; it was more of an "I told you so" quick dip of Roy's chin and eyes.

Hannah leaned against the piano and watched as the busser trudged out of the restaurant. "Did I do the right thing? I didn't even ask him his name. He might be a little slow, but that doesn't mean he doesn't deserve *one* date."

Roy wrinkled his forehead. "Slow?"

Hannah waved a hand in front of her face. "I know what you're thinking, and he was super speedy cleaning up after me tonight. What I meant was …" She scratched the back of her head, wondering if she should disclose how attracted she was to the hairy busser and how she feared she might date him for all the wrong reasons. She clicked her tongue instead of speaking. It was better to let it lie. She pulled a fifty from her waitress's belt and tossed it into Roy's jar, then kissed his cheek. "Thanks for stepping into the fight tonight and always watching out for me."

Roy nodded and produced his signature wide grin. "Wouldn't want to see you get caught with the crocodiles."

She winked, then strolled toward the kitchen, grateful that another grueling shift had ended. She wiggled her toes in her shoes and did a little hop; she couldn't wait for her interview at the Law Offices of Grant and Grant tomorrow.

CHAPTER TWO

*S*imon pulled at his covers, tucking them in under his back to block out the cold. He'd often dreamt of his ergonomic bed and soft pillows while he shimmied around in his stiff African cot the past three months.

Ironically, now that he was finally sleeping in his comfortable bed—after years of subpar mattresses—he couldn't sleep. The cold bite in the air had kept him awake a good portion of last night. No, that was a lie; it wasn't the cold that kept him awake. He'd slept fine the previous three nights, even with jet lag, but during the last several hours, his mind had raced with thoughts of Hannah. He couldn't get the green-eyed beauty out of his head. She was a frustrating dichotomy. She'd said she didn't want to date a rich man, and yet she also wouldn't date a poor busser. What was her deal?

He strained to read the nautical clock on the wall through the darkness. The massive clock resembled something out of *Twenty Thousand Leagues Under the Sea*, resembling an instrument that could plummet to the bottom of the ocean and continue to keep accurate time down to the second. It was worth a small fortune. There were moments, when he'd eaten beetles in the bush of Africa or foraged his way through the rainforests of Brazil, when he'd felt one with the people and nature and forgotten how wealthy his family was. But then, when he'd sit down in an internet café to do his weekly reading to stay abreast of his family's holdings and write a few short recommendations for asset allocation and venture capital investments, it would all come back to him— along with a healthy weekly paycheck for simply spending those few hours on his laptop.

"Alexa, turn on the lights," he said, and his room instantly lit to the dimmest setting. He'd designed the room to resemble the inside of a futuristic submarine yacht, including a fish tank wall, like something he'd seen in an aquarium as a kid. He used to sit on his bed and stare at the gliding fish for hours. The mini sharks, stingrays, and puffer fish had always been his favorite. The room was just as he'd left it the day he'd graduated from high school—with his graduation cap still hanging lopsided on the wall. His mom had since added his graduation caps from Harvard. His room, like his brothers', could've doubled as a luxury apartment; he could live in there for a week without stepping outside his door, which he'd done on a few occasions as a teenager.

He sat up in bed and bowed his head in gratitude. Thanks to the generosity of his grandfather, who'd recently left several million to Simon's nonprofit, he could now pay to have several wells built in remote African villages, bringing clean water to thousands of people. As soon as he stepped into the law firm tomorrow, he'd form another humanitarian arm of the family business so he could transfer the cash. He finally had something to look forward to in this small, snobby town, but what he really looked forward to was his night job, where he'd see the woman who'd stolen his sleep.

He envisioned Hannah walking up a dusty path in Kenya while stepping in time to the merry canticles of the locals. She looked back at him as a loving smile played at her lips, her hair floating in the hot dry air. She raised up her bucket of water, then held it steady on top of her head with one raised arm like the Statue of Liberty holding up her torch.

A photo popped into his mind from his grade school yearbook: a cute girl draped in a green sheet to match her eyes as she held up a torch, her face lit with the smile of an angel. "Hannah *Fields*?" He jumped out of bed and ran to his bookshelf to scour his shelves for his yearbooks, but they weren't there. Her name tag had said Hannah. He rubbed his temples. *Think!* he screamed at himself. Could she be *the* Hannah—the girl Levi had crushed on since they were in grade school together? It seemed plausible. Simon had had a crush on her as well; all the boys had—she was the cutest girl in school—and when there were only three hundred kids in an entire private elementary, middle, and high school combined, cute mattered. They didn't see her as often after she'd transferred schools, but he and his brothers never dared mention Hannah's name out loud for fear that Levi would put laxative in their milk or do something even worse. Since she was two years younger than Simon and she'd never even glanced at him, it had been easy to leave her alone, until now.

Simon threw on his loose cotton pajama pants and sprinted down the hall toward the main library on the other side of the thirty-thousand-square-foot home. If his mom had transferred his books anywhere, they'd be in there. His home was the only thing that he'd ever known his mother to spend any real money on, especially her library—which could be transported next to the renowned library in Admont, Austria, and steal the European library's thunder.

His mother had never been materialistic, but she'd often said that her husband and children should want to come home at night, so she'd allowed each of her seven boys to design their own rooms when they were old enough, her husband had designed his study, and she'd created her library. The house wasn't shaped like your typical rectangular box; it was more of an octagon, where everyone had a two-story suite with amazing mountain and valley views.

His stomach growled when the aroma of freshly baked cinnamon bread reached his nose. That was another thing—his mom always made sure the refrigerator and pantry were stocked, which was no small feat considering she had seven large boys in the six-foot range by the time they were sixteen.

Noticing a light on in the kitchen, Simon took a detour on his way to the library. He stepped into the kitchen to find his mother in her black apron, chock-full of dusty white flour while she pushed a rolling pin across a doughy surface.

"Mom," he laughed out. "What are you doing baking at five in the morning?"

Without looking up from her dough, she pointed to the double ovens. "I decided to bake some cinnamon rolls for breakfast to welcome you boys home. I couldn't sleep. I'm so excited to have all of my boys home today. It's been almost six years since I've had all my children under the same roof." She looked up at him with a bright smile that expressed her complete contentment. She blinked, then gasped. "What happened to your face?"

"Oh, this ugly mug? I was born—"

Her face scrunched with concern. "Don't you dare joke and say you were born like that, because you had the prettiest face of all my babies."

Simon stepped around the kitchen island and pulled his mother into a hug. "Are you telling me that I'm not pretty?"

"Seriously, what happened?"

"You'd be proud of me. I protected a woman's honor last night."

"Oh," she sighed out. "I should've known that was you. I'd heard something about an altercation at the restaurant last night on a group chat."

"You do group chats now? Who are you and what happened to my mother?"

She giggled and squeezed him tight. "I've missed you so much."

He kissed the top of her head, then released his hug and slipped onto a barstool. "Who's home?"

She returned to working on her dough. "Everyone except the twins. They're finishing up finals this morning, then flying in tonight to be here in time for the funeral tomorrow."

"So … Levi flew in last night?"

"Yes! And your father has talked him into relocating here. He'll be leaving the office in LA," she said with a happy sigh while she rolled the dough into a log.

"How'd Dad get him to do that? I thought Levi loved LA."

She tilted her chin down and raised her eyes up and off to the side as if she guarded a secret. "Beats me."

If Levi's transfer to Sun Valley had anything to do with Hannah being back in town, Simon would have to step up his game. "Mom, do you think I look like Sasquatch?"

She wrinkled her forehead with concern, then walked around the island and cupped his face in her floured hands. Her hands smelled like sweet cinnamon and cloves, and her kind brown eyes warmed his chest. "You are absolutely perfect, Simon. No matter how you wear your hair or dress, you'll always be perfect to me because you have a kind heart. That's what matters."

He twisted his lips. "So … you're telling me in a nice way that I *do* look like Sasquatch?"

Her body jiggled with laughter, but she didn't release her grip on his face. "Yeah. I'll text my hairdresser right now and get you in before her first appointment for a cut and shave." She pinched his beard in her fingertips, then lovingly patted his cheek. "Plan on an hour or two."

"An hour or two?" he asked.

She wiped her hands off on her apron, pulled her phone from the front pocket in the bib, sent the text in a matter of seconds, then stepped back to her cinnamon rolls. "No joke. It's going to take a while, and my stylist is a perfectionist."

Simon watched her in silence as she cut the rolls with a white string and placed them gently onto the buttered cookie sheet.

"What woke you?" she asked.

He scratched his neck, deciding what to tell her. "It's weird, but something's nagging me about elementary school. Any ideas where my yearbooks went?"

"You and Levi have always been connected in thought and purpose."

"True."

"He came to me in search of his yearbooks late last night. He said it was to prepare for his ten-year high school reunion next week." She clicked her tongue and pointed an accusatory finger at him. "You missed your reunion two years ago. And everyone missed *you*. When there are only thirty-seven people in your graduating class and someone doesn't show up, there's a void—especially when that *someone* is my perfect boy."

"Did Levi find his yearbooks?"

"Yes." She pushed the cinnamon roll pan to the side and

wiped her hands on the Christmas hand towel that draped over her shoulder, giving him her undivided attention. "Follow me to the library." She linked her arm through his and leaned her head into his shoulder as they walked down the quiet hallway. "There's nothing better than having all of my boys home, even if it is for your grandfather's funeral."

"Was he any better to you these past few years? You didn't mention Grandpa when you came to visit me in Belgium."

She sighed. "Sometimes, when someone passes, you remember the good over the bad." She twisted her lips in thought. "That's what I'm planning on doing."

Simon laughed. "You should've been a politician."

"Don't you dare say that," she scoffed, playfully whacking him on the shoulder. "That's all we need in our family: lawyers *and* politicians. We'd be burned at the stake for sure."

He rubbed his tired eyes and yawned. "Hey, aren't you the one who encouraged us to study law?"

She rubbed her chin as they entered the library. "I can't deny that, but I encouraged you so you'd be able to protect yourselves. There aren't many people out there who don't want to take a piece of what we have. Ofttimes, they don't even realize they're doing it. I'm glad you were able to travel the world to gain a greater understanding of your place in it."

"My *place*?" He furrowed his brows. That comment was the first time he'd ever heard his mother say anything about his family being in a class above anyone else.

"You misunderstand me," she said, pointing to a section of the bookshelf. "I mean your *obligation*."

He shook his head. "You're still speaking in code, Mom."

She released an exasperated sigh, like she used to do when he was young and had done something stupid that had resulted in an injury. "With knowledge and privilege comes responsibility." She reached onto her tiptoes and pulled down a thin school yearbook, the cover blotted in bright primary colors. "I think this one will have what you're looking for."

"How do you know what I'm looking for?"

"I've been your mother for twenty-nine years. Even though it took you a few years of living away from me abroad for *you* to realize who you are, I've always known who my son is. He's the man who saves a damsel in distress."

"You mean I'm perfect?" he teased.

Her face blossomed into a radiant smile. "You're absolutely perfect." She tapped her pointer finger on the yearbook that rested in his hands. "Give Levi a chance. He still needs to understand who *he* is."

Simon's mouth dropped open. "You *do* know what I want," he said, his eyes wide with surprise. He handed her back the yearbook.

"Have you not been listening to a word I've said?" She laughed. "Now come and eat a warm fresh cinnamon roll. Then you need to take a shower before you come back to me clean-shaven and handsome."

He raised an eyebrow. "I thought you said I was perfect."

"Yes. You are perfect, but you're more handsome when you're clean-shaven." She wiggled her eyebrows and whistled. "You just wait and see how she reacts."

"How *who* reacts?" asked Simon with a questioning squint of his eyes.

"I've observed and mothered you since infancy." She tapped on the yearbook again. "And before I was a mother, I was a girlfriend, then a wife and lover."

He wrinkled his face in disgust and held his palms out to her, begging her to stop speaking. "Not going there." He handed her back the yearbook. He didn't need it anymore since she'd affirmed who the Hannah working at the restaurant was. "You answered my question. Now, for that cinnamon roll …"

She smiled, linked her arm through his again, and pulled him toward the kitchen.

A few minutes later, Simon strolled back down the hallway toward his room with his belly satisfied and a smile splitting his face. He stopped outside Levi's door and scratched the back of his head, wondering what exactly his mom had meant when she'd said that she wanted Simon to "give Levi a chance; he still needs to understand who he is."

He cracked the door open and stepped into the cold room. Levi had always kept his room cooler than the rest of his brothers', except for Nate. Nate, being the largest of the men and the most agile, was an NFL football player with the Georgia Patriots based in Atlanta.

Simon cleared his throat and stared into the black space. "Levi, you awake?"

Levi moaned out something from the corner of the room from his bed.

The most difficult thing would be to keep the conversation casual. Simon took a step into the room, took in a deep breath, and said, "Hey, man, I saw Hannah the other day and we hit it off. We're gonna be hanging out."

"Hannah?" asked Levi in a long, groggy voice.

"Yeah. Hannah. You probably don't remember her," Simon said quickly.

"Get out!" Something flew past Simon's shoulder and hit the wall with a thump. Levi had never been known as a happy riser.

"No worries. Just a heads-up that I'll be spending some time with Hannah Fields."

"Hands off. Hannah's mine!" Levi's voice rang out, sharp and clear.

Simon clenched his fists as his adrenaline spiked. Time to leave. He'd spoken his piece, and he needed to vacate Levi's bedroom before something more lethal flew at his head. Levi had played baseball in high school, where he'd pitched balls that would routinely clock in at eighty-seven mph.

Thoughts of Hannah permeated Simon's mind as he sprinted down the hallway to his room to shower. She'd meet a new man at the restaurant tonight—not the lowly busser she refused to date. If it was a wealthy man she wanted, she was about to get him.

CHAPTER THREE

*H*annah sat up straight, with her hands folded in her lap and her legs twisted together at her ankles, in a mammoth chair that belonged in an expensive lodge, not a law office. It wasn't uncommon for Sun Valley's homes and businesses to be decorated in a rustic-cabin style, but this chair was gigantic and made her feel like a little girl, waiting for the dentist to extract her teeth. And that's exactly how she felt as she waited in the reception area of Grant and Grant for her interview with Simon Grant, Senior—like her teeth were about to be yanked out with pliers.

The office looked more like a luxury home than an office. The open foyer had a double winding staircase which appeared to float in the air, allowing for the bottom floor where she sat next to the receptionist's white desk to be completely open.

Get a grip! You aren't nervous waiting on him at the Mandolin, she told herself to calm her nerves and stay her trembling hands and rapid breathing. Why did she feel like she was trying to be something she wasn't? She'd earned her Juris Doctor degree, the same as everyone else had in this office. If she kept telling herself that she had nothing to prove, then maybe she'd believe it. She inhaled slowly through her nose and held the air in her chest for ten seconds before releasing. She repeated her exercise several times before Mr. Grant strolled into the reception area with a wide grin.

"Hannah Fields," he said, extending out his large, thick hand. "I'm glad you applied for our open position."

"Thank you for the opportunity to interview with your firm." She gave his hand a steady shake, then followed him up the stairs.

"Want to know the key to a long life?" he asked.

"What's that?"

"Stairs. My grandfather's office was upstairs; my father's office was downstairs. My grandfather is ninety-five years old and still healthy as an ox."

She cleared her throat. "I'm sorry to hear about your father's passing."

"Thank you." He turned back to her and nodded before continuing up the stairs at a brisk pace. He obviously wanted to live a long life like his grandfather, Alfred Grant.

Like Alfred, all the men in the Grant family had exquisite, large, round, light-blue eyes, void of almost all pigment. She'd gotten to know Alfred on a superficial level from waiting on him at the restaurant. Every time he came in to eat, the other employees scattered in fear. She'd never known Alfred to be harsh, but she'd heard rumors that he was tough on his employees and even tougher on his kids and grandkids. Perhaps he'd mellowed with age. She liked to think of him as the main character of the book *Les Misérables* —a man who hid where he came from while he toiled and sweated to make something of himself. Or was she thinking about herself?

While they walked the long corridor to his office, Hannah glanced in through the open office doors that lined the hall.

In every room, a man somewhere between the ages of forty-five and sixty-five sat at his desk and either talked on the phone or tapped at his computer.

The office held the pleasing scent of expensive cologne; she wouldn't mind being around that smell all day. Men's cologne was so much more agreeable to her senses than the strong tang of women's perfume. If they offered her the position, she'd have to get used to the men's musky scent, because there didn't appear to be a single woman working there; even the front receptionist/intern was male. It would be a huge mental shift for her to be around men all day, considering it had only been her and her mom. Even in college and law school, she'd see her female roommates at times, but more evenings than not, it was just her and her computer.

"Have a seat," he said, motioning to a leather chair at a round table that sat four people.

Hannah sat at the table, set her purse down next to her chair, and glanced out the huge picture window next to the table with a view of the white mountain. "You have a gorgeous view."

"Thank you," he said with a nod. "We built this building with the view in mind." He grabbed his chin, rubbed his cheeks, and spent a few seconds staring out the window. "Anytime I get mentally stuck, wondering how I can get us out of some mess, I stare out this window, and then it comes to me."

"Inspiration?" she asked.

"No," he said with a quick shake of his head. "This view helps me remember my place in the world, as my wife would say. That mountain will stand there forever, but we have a finite number of days on the earth. Every morning, I look out this window and think about how grateful I am for what I've been blessed with—starting with my wife." He snapped his fingers and smiled. "Then the inspiration comes."

Hannah had had a few short conversations with Mr. Grant at the restaurant. She'd heard that he was a cut above most men, but it wasn't until his comment on being grateful that she realized what a humble, good man he really was.

"And I want you to be able to think, Hannah, so you need an office with a view as well."

She shifted uncomfortably in her seat as he sat in the chair across from her. Had he just offered her the job? She pressed her palms into her quivering thighs under the table. "If I *am* offered the position as legal counsel here with Grant and Grant, I will give you my all, sir."

"Very good. Now let's talk salary. This is where we start our new attorneys," he said, sliding a piece of folded paper across the table.

She opened the paper and swallowed hard when she read the astronomically high starting salary. She tapped the paper with her index finger and raised her brows. "This is your *starting* salary?"

"What do you think?" His translucent-blue eyes smiled. "Will you join us here at Grant and Grant?"

"You're offering me the job?" Her speech became rapid. "But you haven't asked me one question yet! What if I'm horrible in court?"

He released a deep, pleasant, rolling baritone laugh. "I knew I liked you. Yes, I'm offering you a job. I've seen your transcripts, read through the references that you provided. I know your work ethic from the restaurant, and I understand the grit that it took to put yourself through school. I believe inundating you with a barrage of questions would be redundant and a waste of time—time that could be better spent reading through litigation notes."

Hannah hopped up and shot a hand across the table. "I will gladly work for you, Mr. Grant. Where do I start?"

He shook her hand, then motioned for her to sit back down. "Just one more thing before I show you to your office."

She slowly returned to her seat. *They already have an office ready for me?* Her mind filled with questions she didn't dare ask. She didn't want to seem flustered, or worse—too eager.

Mr. Grant threaded his fingers together and rested his elbows and forearms onto the table as he leaned forward. "We don't have a policy about interoffice relationships. If you'd like to date someone here in the office, you're welcome to do that."

Hannah swallowed down the lump in her throat and cursed the rising heat in her cheeks. Mr. Grant didn't seem to be talking about himself, but who did he think she'd be dating? The only men that worked there were middle-aged or older, except for the male receptionist, who was a few years younger than her. "I understand, but that should not be a problem, because I've promised myself that I would never date anyone from work. I've seen way too many problems result from those relationships. I have yet to break that rule, and I can promise you right here and now that I never will."

He nodded and stood. "Let me show you to your office."

A few minutes later, Hannah stared out her office window at the breathtaking hills and mountains of Sun Valley. The view wasn't as grand as Mr. Grant's, but it was a close second. The office was about ten feet square with a glass desk and a black desktop computer. Taped to the computer screen with clear tape was an instruction sheet on how to log on to Wi-Fi and other similar instructions. Next to the login sheet was a stack of manila folders.

She picked up the top folder and leafed through it. It didn't take her long to realize that the printer had been low on ink when the documents had been printed; they were barely legible. She reviewed the contents of the next folder, then the next. Every file was patchy and unreadable. She lifted the stack of folders and left her office in search of the person who'd copied them, most likely a legal assistant in one of the offices on the first floor. Before she could do anything, she needed to get her hands on copies that were more legible, or even the digital files. She guessed most of the attorneys in the office preferred a printed version, but she was okay with reviewing them in electronic form.

Her heels clicked against the hardwood floor as she went in search of the legal intern. She didn't wear heels often; in fact, the red patent leather stilettos were her mom's. When Mr. Grant had been at her side less than twenty minutes earlier, walking her down that same hallway, his heavy footsteps had drowned out her shoe clicks.

As she passed the other attorneys' offices, each man turned his head and nodded to her in greeting. When she reached the double stairs, she decided to remove her shoes and walk down the stairs barefoot, avoiding a serious tumble. What she really didn't want to do was embarrass herself the first day on the job by falling down the elegant stairs and winding up in the emergency room.

With the stack of folders in one arm, she had to lift her leg and remove her shoes with her free hand. The first shoe came off without a hitch, but the second shoe suctioned to her foot. She noticed two tall, well-built men walking through the lobby below her. They were both dressed in suits and strutted through the office like they owned it. Maybe she'd spoken too soon when she'd told Mr. Grant she'd never date a fellow attorney at the law firm. With one foot still lifted off the ground, she hopped over to the railing to sneak another glance at the handsome men before they disappeared under the stairwell.

Hannah stumbled and hit the railing with a thump,

causing the two men to stop and look up at her. She recognized one of them as Levi. Her mind raced with ways to play the awkward moment off. She acted nonchalant—as if she'd never stumbled and smacked into the railing at all. "Hey," she said with a smile, but the momentum of her body hitting the railing caused the manila folders in arms to jettison into the air. "Oh no!" she gasped as dozens of loose white sheets of paper flew over the railing and slowly floated down like feathers in a pillow fight.

Luckily, floating papers didn't make any noise. At least the entire office hadn't run out into the foyer to witness Hannah's mortification.

Levi grabbed a few papers out of the air as they fell to him, and he smiled mischievously at her. "That was almost as good as when you stole Mark Carter's clothes from the watering hole when he and his buddies went skinny-dipping." He threw his head back and laughed. "Where *did* they find those poison ivy plants to cover up with?"

"Beats me." She laughed, descending the stairs. "Those boys had no business stripping down so we wouldn't get in. I'm surprised you remember that."

He grabbed the last of the floating papers out of the air. "I remember a lot more about you than that. I was just headed out to grab some coffees for the office and could use another set of hands."

Hannah walked up to the two men and started helping them gather the papers. Levi's associate didn't look up at her, but when she saw his profile, her heart raced; he was gorgeous. *Why did I say I wouldn't date a co-worker?* She wanted to kick herself.

She turned back to Levi. "Didn't you see how clumsy I can be? Are you sure you want me carrying cups of coffee?"

The man with the handsome profile laughed from his

bent position as he continued to pick up the scattered papers.

Levi adjusted his tie as he stepped in front of his associate. "From what I've heard, you're the best waitress at the Mandolin, even if you're assigned a subpar busser. You don't get praised like that if you're clumsy."

She found that to be an odd statement. Why would he care about a busser? "I wouldn't say subpar. The busser last night did a great job, and he got a shiner protecting me. It's just so nice to see that your family is still employing people who are slow."

"Slow?" The man next to Levi jumped up from his bent position and blinked his big brown eyes, one of which was black and blue and swollen.

Hannah's hand flew to her mouth. Her speech muffled as she spoke through her fingers. "You're the busser? I don't understand."

He pointed to himself. "What *I* don't understand is how you could call me slow. I busted my butt last night running after you."

Levi raised an eyebrow. "Maybe she doesn't want you to run after her."

Hannah sensed competitiveness between them. "I didn't mean it like that. I thought you were *mentally* slow." She placed her hand over her mouth again, but this time she held it firmly in place. She couldn't be trusted to say another word.

Levi slapped the guy on the back and laughed. "She thinks you're slow."

She scrunched her forehead in apology and slowly dropped her hands at her side. "No. I don't think you're slow. Last night I thought you must've been slow because of how young you were to be bussing tables, your scruffy appearance, and ..." She looked him up and down. Dang, he

29

cleaned up nicely. He was attractive last night, but now that his large eyes and full lips were visible, he was drop-dead gorgeous. She tilted her head to the side and stared at him.

Levi coughed. "What were you saying about his scruffy appearance, Hannah?"

She blinked to stop herself from staring. "He's not scruffy anymore."

The tall, gorgeous man took a step closer to her, narrowing the space between them. "No. And I'm also not just a busser."

"I can see that, but that's not why I wouldn't …" This was awkward. "I thought you were slow."

"I'm not," he said with a smile that made her weak in the knees. He held his hand out to her in greeting. "I'm Simon."

Everything was starting to make sense. It pained her to think of how she'd responded to him last night. "Simon?" she asked, giving his hand a quick shake. "As in Simon Grant, Junior?"

He bowed slightly. "At your service."

Levi snapped his fingers. "We need to be at the *service* desk of the coffee shop in five minutes, or the drinks I ordered will be cold." He lightly touched Hannah's arm. "Will you come help me, Hannah? Simon can finish gathering up these papers."

She shook her head. "I can't let Simon clean up my mess, and definitely not alone."

Simon looked at his brother with a cocked eyebrow. "She wants to stay with me."

Levi squared his shoulders and breathed out through his nose like a bull. This strange standoff was something that caused the inner peacemaker in her to surface.

"Okay," she said. "Simon, why don't you join us? I'm sure we could use more hands. Right, Levi? These papers will just take a minute for all of us to pick up."

The young office intern stepped out of an office at the end of the hall with a look of horror on his face. "I'll get this," he said, reaching down and carefully retrieving the papers from off the floor as if they'd just committed genocide in the foyer, *his* foyer. Good thing he wasn't there when Hannah had dropped the papers, or he might not ever print a copy or run an errand for her in the future. "Whose office do these papers go back in?"

Levi and Simon looked at Hannah.

Hannah cleared her throat. "No office. Just shredded." She breathed out a sigh of relief when the intern shrugged, then resumed picking up the papers.

They exited the building to a clear, sunny morning. The weather station had said that it would be close to sixty-five degrees today, the hottest day of the year so far, and Hannah was in heaven. She marveled, not only at the beauty of the peaceful little alcove of Sun Valley during off-season—or slack, as the locals called it—but also that she now had a good-paying job and her best childhood friend back. She found it odd that she felt so comfortable around Levi after such a long stretch of time, but it was like they were kids again, running and jumping in the swimming hole together.

Simon, on the other hand, made her feel uncomfortable in so many ways. She'd need to keep some distance between them to figure out what was happening with her mind, and her body, every time their eyes met.

CHAPTER FOUR

*S*imon kept his head down as he shoveled a forkful of scrambled eggs into his mouth. If he stared at his white porcelain plate and ignored the conversation around him, then his brothers wouldn't bug him about his black eye or increasingly bad attitude; to say he was mad, disappointed, and frustrated would be to downplay his irritation.

The culprit responsible for Simon's irritation, Levi, sat at the other end of the long sixteen-person table in their mother's formal dining room, scarfing down his hash browns. With the amount of food their family chef had prepared that morning at their mother's instruction, Simon and his brothers wouldn't be hungry for a good part of the day—or at least not during their grandfather's funeral, which started in an hour.

Simon seethed as he gulped down his orange juice. He wasn't usually as grouchy as Levi in the mornings, but with the minimal sleep he'd gotten the last two nights and with how upset he'd become with the situation with Hannah and Levi, he knew all it would take was the wrong look from one of his brothers to set him off.

He couldn't get Hannah out of his mind. She'd ignored him during their coffee run, which had been a complete last-minute concoction by Levi to spend time with her. Simon had to hand it to his crafty brother; he was a quick thinker. Simon could see why Levi flourished as the family's leading defense attorney in LA. It was a lofty task to defend the family's holdings and venture capitalist interests, and he'd heard that Levi excelled in that arena.

After they'd returned to the office yesterday, Simon continued to try to get Hannah's attention with every advance he'd *thought* he'd perfected over his past decade of dating, but nothing had worked; she hadn't given him the time of day. Why was this one girl, who he thought he knew so well, so difficult to please?

"Thank you," said Simon as one of the house staff he didn't recognize set down a platter of bacon in front of him and refilled his glass of orange juice. He'd forgotten about all the comforts of home; his mother had every intention of reminding her sons how good they would have it if they moved back home. There was one brother Simon hoped *wouldn't* stay. "Levi, when are you headed back to LA?"

The other brothers stopped talking and looked between them.

Levi laughed. "No plans. Does that mess up *your* plans? I heard about your lost bet."

Simon shrugged, unsuccessfully playing off how much Levi's comment stung. "I'm just here for the foundation. Then I'll move on."

Levi threw down his cloth napkin. "And that's *exactly* why you're no good for Hannah!"

Simon jumped to his feet, causing his chair to shoot back and hit the wall with a loud bang. He hadn't meant to be that dramatic, but he'd roll with it. "You have no idea what's good for Hannah!" he shouted back.

"And you think *you* do?" Levi asked in a mocking tone. "What a joke."

Simon caught a glimpse of green being slapped on the table as he strutted across the room toward Levi—the bet was on.

"My money's on Levi," said John to his identical twin, Tom.

"You're on," replied Tom, tossing another bill onto the table.

The age-old family tradition of betting on a brother's fight, which had happened on almost a daily basis in their home growing up, took shape as green bills stacked up in an uneven pile in the center of the table. Simon couldn't back down, not now that bets had been placed.

"You're meat," spat Simon with the twitch of his nose and a growl.

"Don't you mean you're *dead* meat?" replied Levi with attitude as he widened his stance and squared his shoulders.

Levi was right, which fueled Simon's anger. His English grammar had suffered over the last few years, beginning three years ago when he'd embarked on the self-actualization part of his journey by immersing himself in the local culture and speaking the native language for a season.

Simon had had enough of Levi's attitude. *I'm gonna wipe that pretentious grin ...* His mind gave him justification to throw the first punch. His knuckles connected with Levi's obnoxious mouth. Less than two seconds later, Simon found himself against the wall with a sucker punch to his gut. He cursed when the wind blew out from his lungs, causing him to gasp for air. Simon grabbed Levi's head and placed it into a headlock, pulling him out of the dining area and into the large open area of the living room—their favorite area to wrestle in as kids because, other than the enormous L-sectioned couch that faced the television on the wall, the thousand-square-foot area was free of any breakable obstacles.

Their fight continued onto the floor until the familiar smell of roses caused them to both freeze in their tangled position. "Stop!" screamed their mom as she stomped into the living room. Her expression said that if the two of them weren't already bloody and sore, she'd finish the task.

"Don't stress," said Simon. "We were just messing around." Now that he and Levi had had it out, his frustrations had abated.

Their mother's eyes narrowed in on Simon with a death glare. "Follow me to the study, please."

Simon pointed at himself. "What makes you think *I* started this?" He cast a glance at Levi, who was pointing to his fat lip. Simon laughed, then tilted his head back, lifting his chin to Levi in defiance. "Serves you right." He turned and followed his mother down the hall to the library. He'd acted like a child, but sometimes he found that acting like a child in the confines of his own home was the best therapy.

When they reached the study, she motioned for Simon to close the French glass doors behind him. "I thought I'd asked you to give Levi a chance."

"You might need to give me more direction there."

She stared him down until he caved.

He blew out a frustrated breath. "Okay, I'll back off. But I don't understand why. And Hannah won't give me the time of day, anyway."

His mother sat in the leather love seat and patted the cushion next to her for him to sit. Simon obeyed, but tried to look away.

"I need you to trust me, Simon," she said. "You have my eyes and, unfortunately, my stubborn personality."

"What outcome are you hoping for here, Mom?"

She took his face in her hands, which were callused from her many years of tending to her horses, and kissed his forehead. "I want you to be happy, son." She twisted her lips and furrowed her brow, watching him intently. Then her face relaxed and she smiled. "Not fleeting happiness. You deserve a lifetime of happy moments with someone you love."

"And you think Levi will find that with Hannah? And I'll find that someday with someone else?"

"I didn't say that," she said with a slow blink. "Trust me. Take a step back."

She wanted him to roll the dice, but what was she betting on exactly? He scratched his chin. "Do I hear a bet in there?"

She laughed. "No way. This doesn't need a bet. It only needs a little—"

"Patience." He finished her sentence with a deflated sigh. He wasn't looking forward to sitting back and watching the woman of his dreams fall in love with his brother, but it didn't look like he had much choice. He painfully swallowed down his pride as he stood to go find Levi.

Five minutes later, Simon stepped into Levi's bedroom. It was like walking into a billiard room in a European castle. A crystal chandelier hung over a billiard table in the center of the room, surrounded by tan couches and Victorian paintings framed in gold. Levi stood in front of an antique-bronze Cheval mirror, adjusting his tie.

"I'm bowing out," said Simon, leaning against Levi's open doorframe.

Scrutinizing his reflection in the mirror, Levi threw Simon a sideways glance. "You're not just saying that so I'll be unprepared when you strike and sabotage?"

Simon raised an eyebrow. "Strike and sabotage? Not my

MO." He stared at Levi's swollen lip. "Ouch, what happened to your lip?"

"I fell," Levi said flatly, until he couldn't hold a straight face any longer and laughed. He turned away from his reflection in the mirror to look at Simon. "Truce?"

"Truce," echoed Simon, barreling into Levi with a big brother hug.

Brothers once more. *Now* Simon was home.

CHAPTER FIVE

a cold hand pressed into Hannah's back between her shoulder blades as she ascended the stone steps of the old white A-framed church, built in the late 1800s. "Stand straight," her mother instructed.

Hannah instinctively puffed out her chest and sucked in her tummy. "We're going to a funeral, Mom. This isn't a social gathering for me to find a husband." Her thoughts went to Simon's lips and strong jawline.

"Can you imagine the wealth that'll be in this room in an hour, darling?" Her mother's voice grew giddy.

"Are you thinking about someone for me?" Hannah raised a brow. "Or for yourself?"

She answered Hannah's question with the tsk of her tongue and a dismissive flick of her wrist while they took their seats on the slick, wooden pew four rows back from the front. The first three rows on either side of the center aisle were roped off for family members of the deceased. Hannah's mother had insisted they arrive at least forty-five minutes early, because now that Hannah worked for the

Grants, she was practically family and needed to act accordingly.

The church smelled like burnt vanilla candles and old, wet wood. Hannah pulled her phone from her purse to check her email.

"Put that thing away!" her mother chastised. "You don't want everyone thinking you're a Millennial."

Hannah cast her mother a confused glance. "I *am* a Millennial."

"Only chronologically speaking, but that's why you need to marry a rich man. Millennials will be the downfall of this great country."

Hannah laughed. "You don't have to be so dramatic." She almost continued the conversation by noting that her mother had married a rich man, and look how much good that had done them—and if the destruction of Millennials was coming, her mother was partly to blame, because she'd made and raised one, adding to the country's "downfall." Hannah held her tongue out of respect—and because that she didn't want to start an argument in a church as they awaited a funeral service.

A chorus of rough, deep voices echoed from the hall that ran the length of the chapel on the other side of the wall where Hannah sat. She smiled to herself; it sounded as if the choir boys had been replaced with husky men. She followed the men's heavy footsteps and muffled voices as they walked up the hallway. The other mourners in the chapel didn't seem to notice the men until the Grant brothers entered the chapel from a side door at the front of the chapel, next to the pulpit.

Her mother nudged Hannah in the side with her elbow. "Look at all of that hunky husband material."

Hannah's cheeks burned. She and her mother were no longer alone in the chapel, and she felt familiar ears leaning in. In a community of less than 3,000, everyone knew everyone's business. "Shh," she shushed her mother.

"The tall, dark one is looking at you," her mother continued, obviously not worried about what the neighbors would think about matchmaking her daughter to a billionaire during a funeral.

Hannah's attention shot to where her mother was looking and locked eyes with Simon. He nodded to her serenely, then did the same to everyone else in the congregation who seemed to catch his eye. He spoke into one of his brothers' ears, then slipped into the corridor. Hannah's heart dropped, but she had no claim on him. Simon wasn't hers, and he never would be. He obviously thought of her like every other plain Jane out there. And this *was* his grandfather's funeral. He was there to mourn, not flirt with women.

"That one's looking at you too," her mother said with excitement.

"Mom, please," Hannah said through a locked jaw, her lips barely moving. She refused to look up again.

Her mom tapped her arm incessantly. "He's coming over here."

When a man's footsteps reached her side, Hannah slowly raised her eyes to find Levi smiling down at her.

"Hannah, Ms. Fields," he said quietly. "Please come join us." He offered his hand to Hannah. "Beautiful women should never sit alone."

"Nor beautiful men," her mother said, nudging Hannah as if she should've returned the compliment.

Hannah swallowed to relieve her instant dry mouth. She took Levi's hand and stood. "Thank you, Levi. We'd love to join your family." She glanced back at her mother with eyes that pleaded for her to stop talking.

Levi opened the rope that restricted access to the first pew and motioned for them to take a seat at the end of the bench. "I'll be back in a few minutes," he said quietly, then disappeared out of the room like the rest of his brothers after Simon had walked back out.

Her mother elongated her neck and sat with the elegance of a queen, or at least someone who played the part of a queen. Her mother had spunk, with her jet-black, pixie-cut hairstyle and heavy black eyeliner that caused her vibrant blue eyes to sparkle like sapphires. Hannah sighed; her mother had always been, and always would be, gorgeous. She expected that one day her mother would run away to LA or New York to be an actress. She had a theatrical flair. She'd hobnobbed with several movie producers, actors, and screenwriters over the years who'd come into town for some quality R&R and to rub shoulders with other people in the entertainment industry. Her mom had become acquainted with some of the regulars and considered them to be friends. Hannah doubted whether the connection was as reciprocal as her mother had described, but she found that if she encouraged her mother and acted interested, it made her mother happy—so that's exactly what she did.

The congregation shuffled to their feet, giving their attention to the back of the chapel. With the positive energy in the air, it felt as if they should be standing for a bride walking down the aisle, not a funeral procession. The casket entered on the shoulders of the pallbearers from the back of the chapel. A hush settled over the chapel as the casket made its way up the aisle with Simon and Levi, the eldest grandsons, holding up the head of the casket. Hannah bowed her head, not necessarily out of reverence, but because she had no idea where to look; every few seconds, either Simon or Levi would make eye contact with her. She found their attention unnerving. She'd almost convinced herself that the Grant men were merely natural observers. Perhaps no one had told them when they were younger that staring wasn't socially acceptable.

"I'd guess either one of those strapping young men would date you," said her mother.

Would date me? Hannah wanted to scream. Instead, she nodded and smiled sweetly at her mother, hoping that if she acquiesced, her mother would finally drop it.

After the men set the casket onto the stand in front of the pulpit, they dispersed to their seats, with Levi making a beeline for Hannah's row. Before the preacher began his speech, the front rows filled with Grants.

Hannah leaned into Levi's ear. "You have a big family," she whispered.

Levi lifted half of his face as if he wanted to smile but the circumstances wouldn't allow it. "Close family friends. Come bowling at the lodge tonight with us, and you can meet the ones we grew up with."

Hannah studied the faces of the newcomers who sat in the Grant family rows at the front of the church. She tried to remember meeting any of them, but she drew a blank. Living in a vacation town where at any given day there were more skiers walking the streets than residents, these family friends could have come every year and she'd never have known. She glanced around the chapel as the officiator began his speech. Other than the first three rows, she recognized everyone else in the chapel. Not only did she know them from school and social gatherings; many locals also frequented the Mandolin restaurant.

"Would you want to come?" Levi asked.

She hadn't realized that he was waiting for an immediate response with the funeral in full swing. "I'd love to. What time?"

"I can pick you up at six."

Was he asking her out on a date during his grandfather's

funeral? There were several things unsettling about the idea of dating Levi, one being his brother who now sat across the aisle from them. She glanced over at Simon, and he smiled, causing her heart to race. "You have a lot to worry about today with your guests and the after services, Levi. Don't worry about me. I'm good to meet you guys there at six."

Levi scratched his forehead and nodded. Her response didn't seem to appease him.

The preacher welcomed Levi's father up to the pulpit to give a life's sketch of his father. Mr. Grant's depiction of his father was both factual and sentimental; he didn't bash his father for being absentee, but nor did he exalt him. Hannah had never enjoyed a funeral until now, sitting next to her old childhood buddy and listening to the interesting life of his grandfather and how his example had helped shape Mr. Grant, her new boss.

Levi raised a tissue to his nose. Hannah hadn't recognized Levi's fragile emotional state until that moment. She scooted over so that their sides touched, then placed her hand on top of his and squeezed. "I'm sorry for your loss, Levi." At least she could give him the comfort of a friend's touch.

"Thanks," he said softly, reaching across his body with his free hand and cupping the side of her face. He pulled her in gently until her head rested against his shoulder.

In her mind, she was giving him a sideways hug of comfort, but she started to wonder what he was thinking when his fingertips lightly caressed the back of her hand. Her body tensed and she prayed that the services would end soon. She had no idea how to disengage her physical support from Levi now that she'd given it to him. After a few minutes of internal planning, she slowly lifted her head and tilted it to the side, pretending to listen intently to the next person who stood to speak about Levi's grandfather. The speaker, a middle-aged man with thick white hair and a debonair smile only seen in the movies, was one of the family friends she didn't recognize.

Hannah needed to now figure out a way to pull back her hand. When the speaker finished his thoughts, she snuck a peek at Simon and their eyes locked. He slowly closed one eye into a hard wink. His mother, who sat next to him on the bench, discreetly elbowed him in the gut—but Hannah caught their exchange. Hannah's heart sped violently until *her* mother elbowed her in the side, causing her stomach to flip. Unfortunately, her mother had also caught Simon's wink —and Hannah and Levi's hand-holding.

During the next ten minutes of eulogy, Hannah avoided her mother's inquisitive stare. She tried to convince herself that Levi and Simon were simply overly friendly guys who sought out extra support from friends and family at this difficult time of loss. It would be silly to think that they both wanted to date her.

When the services concluded, she was as confused as ever. She wished she hadn't accepted Levi's offer to go bowling with his family and friends that evening, but how could she cancel on him now that she'd already committed ... and on a day of mourning?

CHAPTER SIX

*H*annah walked into the bowling alley in the basement of Sun Valley lodge to a chorus of laughter. It looked like a game of bowling could chase away the blues, and it smelled like it too. It sure did the trick for Hannah when she smelled the tantalizing aroma of gourmet hamburgers.

The bowling alley must have gotten a face-lift since she'd been there last; the gold and red painted diamonds on the walls shimmered brighter than she'd remembered, and the six bowling lanes, sectioned off in twos, were slightly longer. But it still held its old-time charm. It was one of the oldest bowling alleys in the west, and Hannah had always loved the relaxed atmosphere there. This was a place someone could escape the high-society functions and enjoy a good laugh with close friends.

"Hannah!" exclaimed Levi as he placed a fluorescent green bowling ball onto the mechanical lane runner with a wide grin.

She couldn't help but grin back at his enthusiasm. "Hey,

there." She walked to him at farthest lane against the back wall. "Sorry I'm a few minutes late."

"No worries. We're just choosing our alter-ego names. What'll yours be?"

"Hmm ..." she said. "How about Fly Girl?"

Levi snapped his fingers and pointed to her before typing her name into the computer. "That's right. We used to call you fly girl because you caught the most fish fly fishing. Do you still fish?"

"I haven't for ages, but I'm excited to finally have time again."

"Let me introduce you to our close family friends." He motioned to two men and a woman with her nose in a book, who sat on the cherry-red vinyl stools on the next lane over. "Hannah, this is Annie, Kai, and Zee."

The two men stood and held out their hands in greeting. Hannah smiled and gave them a quick shake. They were both attractive; their eyes were the color of tropical turquoise waters and their skin tone was a light, golden-brown.

"Luckily both of these guys are now married, so women will now finally give me a second glance," Levi teased.

Zee, the taller one, put his arm around Levi. "This guy has a heart of gold." He patted Levi's chest. "Too bad he's right about the women, though," he said with a laugh. "They've always found me irresistible."

"Irresistibly *annoying*," said Annie as she dropped the book on the tall table behind her and jumped from her stool in one fluid movement, like she was leaping into the air like a ballerina. She put her arms around Hannah and squeezed tight. "I can tell that we're going to be good friends, Hannah."

"Are these your brothers?" asked Hannah. She'd always wanted siblings.

Zee laughed. "She's an adopted kid sister and plays the part fabulously. Don't you think?"

Annie narrowed her eyes at Zee. "I married their cousin, Paxton. He's watching our little girl over by the arcade games right now." She pointed to the dining/arcade area. "We're switching off games with who gets the little cutie—like Zee and his wife, Tori, are doing."

Hannah suddenly felt like she was on a double date with Levi and his married friends. Surprisingly, she didn't feel the normal awkwardness that came along with a first date that involved other married couples.

"Let's get this party started," said Levi, clapping his hands. "Zee, you're up."

Zee grabbed his ball as Levi handed Hannah her bowling shoes. She sat down on the stool next to Annie and took off her Vans.

"How do your families know each other?" Hannah asked Kai as he held out his hands to take her shoes.

"Levi's grandfather provided the initial funding for our father's Silicon Valley tech business with Grant venture capital seed money."

Levi nodded. "In turn, Kai and Zee's dad made the Grant Corporation a lot of money, enough to invest in other ventures and roll the dice, again and again."

Kai raised an eyebrow. "A lot of luck."

"And brains." Levi patted Kai on the shoulder. "You're not going to find many guys smarter or more successful than Kai Terrence."

Zee bowled a strike, then pointed to himself. "Excuse me? Who's the successful one here?"

Hannah smiled. She loved how Levi and his friends gave each other a hard time.

"I'll put these away," said Kai with a laugh as he ran off with Hannah's street shoes.

"Levi, you're up," said Zee.

Hannah swiveled her stool around to face Annie. Annie's

appearance was still perfectly polished, like she'd appeared at the funeral; her blond hair was in soft curls and her shimmery gold eye shadow and black eyelashes brought out the golden streaks in her hazel eyes. Hannah pictured Annie more comfortable in a secondhand bookstore without any makeup, curled up in a worn 1970s orange-and-brown-striped oversized chair with her hair up in a messy bun and not a care in the world.

"I knew we'd get along," Annie said with a smile and a wink.

Hannah had been caught staring, but that didn't explain why everyone was winking at her today. "I can't imagine you not getting along with anyone," said Hannah. "What are you reading?"

Annie held up her hardcover book. *"For Whom the Bell Tolls* by Ernest Hemingway. I could recite for you any section of *The Old Man and the Sea*, but I'd never read *For Whom the Bell Tolls*. Minutes before our flight, while researching what to do here in Sun Valley, I learned that Hemingway wrote part of *For Whom the Bell Tolls* while staying in this lodge. He later returned and finished up his final edits here."

And he didn't pay a dime to stay here, Hannah complained internally. Why was it that rich and famous people never had to pay for anything? Hemingway's estate, which the local library now owned, was a quiet ten-minute walk up the country road from Hannah's home. She'd known all about the acclaimed author—nearly every person in Ketchum could moonlight as an Ernest Hemingway tour guide—but Hannah wasn't his biggest fan. It had nothing to do with her disliking his macho literary works. In fact, she hadn't read most of them. Hemingway reminded her of her own father, a man who'd cheated on his first wife with his soon-to-be second, then repeated the cycle over and over again. Perhaps someday she could separate Hemingway's accomplishments from his immoral personal life, but not today, not yet.

"You okay?" asked Annie. "You seem troubled about something."

Hannah blinked, reminding herself to stay in the present. No good came from reliving past heartaches—and her parents' divorce was one big heartache. "I'm not a huge Hemingway fan."

Annie's face dropped.

"Sorry. I didn't mean to offend you."

Annie waved a hand in the air. "It'll take a lot more than that to offend me. I wish my critical reviews were as gentle as 'I'm not a huge fan.'"

"Reviews?" asked Hannah. "Are you an author?"

Annie lifted a pen in the air and clicked it. "I was in my former life. I wrote romance for several years." She pulled her hair up into a quick, messy bun, then stuck her pen into the top. That was more like how Hannah envisioned Annie.

Putting her dislike for Hemingway aside, Hannah drew on her Hemingway trivia. "Did you know that *For Whom the Bell Tolls* was nominated for a Pulitzer the year it was released, but the committee later decided not to award a Pulitzer for fiction that year?" Hannah waggled her eyebrows. "Rumor has it that the Dean of Cambridge and overseer of the Pulitzer awards strongly advocated to have the book *not* receive the award because of the steamy romance."

"No!" Annie's mouth dropped open. She regained her composure, slid closer to Hannah, and said, "Something tells me one provocative scene wouldn't preclude anyone from receiving the Pulitzer these days. In fact, it probably wouldn't even get mentioned if it didn't have a little spice in there. Personally, I'm retired from romance. My last project was a historical fiction novel about another woman named Hannah, but she was from World War II Germany."

"You said you wrote in a *former* life?"

"Before the birth of my beautiful baby girl. I don't have a lot of time to write these days, chasing after my energetic toddler, but I scribble down my thoughts to keep the juices flowing. I've seen what happens to artists who stop creating." She widened her eyes, appearing fearful. "And it ain't pretty."

Hannah smiled at Annie's playful expression.

"Did I hear someone say something ain't pretty over here?" Levi handed Hannah a bowling ball. "Because from where I'm standing, there ain't nothin' *but* pretty right here in front of me."

"Ahh," Annie cooed, patting Levi on his arm. "They don't get much sweeter than you." She turned and winked at Hannah again. "Lucky girl."

Annie must have assumed that she and Levi were a couple, but why wouldn't she? Hannah had sat with Levi in the family section at the funeral, and now she was spending the evening laughing with his close family friends. She enjoyed reconnecting with Levi, but she didn't feel comfortable with people assuming they were a couple—and Levi not setting them straight.

Hannah took the bowling ball from Levi's hands. "Thanks," she said, ignoring his intense gaze. "This bowling ball feels heavier than I'm used to, but I'll *roll* with it." She threw her arm back to gain momentum to throw the ball. As her body naturally turned, she winked over at Annie and Levi to exaggerate the pun. Who knew winks could be contagious?

Simon walked up behind Annie just in time to catch Hannah's wink. He winked back, his face lifting into a seductive smile. Electricity shot through her, causing her brain to scramble like opposing electrons bouncing off each other haphazardly. As if she was struck with a sudden bout of amnesia, she forgot she was bowling. Instead of releasing the ball when she should have, her fingers clutched the inside of the moist, warm holes, sticky with fresh sweat. The heavy ball pulled her forward by her outstretched arm, causing her to hop a few feet into the bowling lane. When the smooth leather bottoms of her bowling shoes hit the slick floor of the lane, she began slipping, which, in turn, caused her feet to shuffle like she was doing a little dance from the 1920s. The ball slid from her fingers and flew forward, bouncing a few times before it rolled down the lane and knocked down every pin.

The entire bowling alley—the six full lanes of Levi's brothers and close friends—clapped and laughed at Hannah's unlikely success. Before turning back to her bowling buddies, she bowed her head in embarrassment and cursed the rising heat in her cheeks, which would broadcast to everyone just how uncoordinated and inept she felt.

Levi grabbed her by her waist. "That was amazing!"

She put on her most convincing happy face, then turned and smiled up at him. "Thanks, but I think I may need a lighter ball. I'll be right back." She quickly slipped away, escaping to a corner of the bowling alley where the balls were lined neatly on color-coded racks. In that desolate corner, she hoped to regain her composure. She leaned against the black-and-white checker-painted wall with her back to the bowling lanes and pretended to scan the rack of bowling balls. She hid her rosy cheeks, hid her rapid breath, and hid her flustered body from Simon, the man who caused her mind and body to forget the simplest things.

"Can I help you choose a ball?" asked Simon, stepping in front of her.

She sucked in a nervous breath and pressed an open palm to her chest. "You scared me to death," she lied. Her rapid breath wasn't from fear. Or maybe it was—fear of how this guy acted like the photon to her electron. Having Simon this close to her was like trying handle a junior high school science experiment that was exploding. As a photon, Simon's photoelectric energy caused her little electron mind to emit and burst random signals throughout her body. Whoever postulated that attraction was chemically based was a genius.

He laughed. "Sorry. I didn't mean to scare you, but I'm really good at choosing bowling balls based on height and weight—but I'm not sure that's what you need."

She knitted her eyebrows together. "Didn't you see that spectacle? I think a new bowling ball is *exactly* what I need."

"You stole the show tonight. After the emotionally taxing week we've had, believe me, you are *exactly* what this family needs."

"I am?" She pointed to herself. "You and your brothers are just fine without me."

"I beg to differ." His eyes shot in Levi's direction; then he turned his back to her and palmed the balls on their stand until he lifted out a bright orange one. "I'm not the best at stepping back," he said, mostly to himself. "Levi's waiting for you."

She didn't take the ball. Instead, her hand flew to her hip. "Levi and I aren't a couple. Why does everyone keep assuming we are?"

"Because Levi would like you to be." He placed the bowling ball back on its stand. "Isn't it obvious? And you don't seem to be dissuading his advances in any way." Simon's body tensed. "You snuggle up to him during his grandfather's funeral, then you let him hold your waist." His words had an acidic tang to them, fueling her anger.

"And what? Everyone's decided to match me up with Levi? Don't I have a say in this? What if it's *you* I want to kiss?" She poked her index finger into his rock-hard chest, then slapped her hand to her mouth—her big, fat, stupid mouth. Hannah refused to meet Simon's gaze. Instead, she stared straight ahead, watching his chest rise and fall with increasing energy.

Simon's fingers curled around her hand that covered her mouth, causing goose bumps to flow down her arm. He slowly pulled her hand away from her lips and held it to his chest over his heart, as if he planned to pull her into a slow dance. "You want to kiss *me*?" he asked in a deep, sultry voice.

She took in a long breath, then released a nervous sigh while raising her eyes to meet his. His caramel-brown irises held her captive. He was no longer a photon; he was now a proton that pulled her in. She felt powerless as his face slowly lowered and his focus shifted to her lips.

Her body tingled with anticipation, and she wondered if his body did as well. Her chest crackled like glowing embers longing to be stoked—until his warm moist lips draped over hers, causing her chest to light on fire. He'd entranced her mind and broken through her walls, annulling any and all reservations she'd ever had about participating in public displays of affection. She didn't care where they were or who saw them; all she cared about was how amazing it felt to kiss Simon Grant. She tilted her head to the side and pressed her back into the wall for support in case she fainted, which was a very real possibility. She ran her hands up his crisp linen shirt until she reached his neck. Her fingertips traced his Adam's apple, then ran along his masculine, square jaw. She felt him holding back from her, and she wanted more; she needed more. She clutched the back of his neck and pulled him closer, deepening their kiss. He responded to her enthusiasm with rugged and reckless zeal, causing a burst of heat to flow through her veins like swift-moving lava down an established channel, reaching highway speeds.

Mid-kiss, Simon pulled back. "I can't do this. I promised. Excuse me, Hannah."

Before Hannah could process what he'd said, he was gone, leaving her to blink away the stars he'd placed in her eyes. She held up a finger. "What just happened?" she asked herself.

Someone cleared their throat, prompting her to turn around. There stood Annie, holding a small notepad in the air. "Would you like me to read it back to you? Wow, I didn't know Simon had that in him." She teetered from side to side. "Well, I thought it a possibility ... you know, with all his macho-ness."

Hannah's cheeks flushed and her mouth dropped open. If Simon hadn't just run away from her, then maybe she wouldn't have been quite so embarrassed. But he hadn't merely run from her; he'd sprinted in the opposite direction. "You saw us kissing?"

Annie tapped the notepad with her pen. "Let me read this back to you and see if I got it right."

"Hannah, it's your ball!" yelled Levi from their lane.

Hannah's eyes bulged. "Levi," she whispered to Annie as if she'd been caught cheating on Levi. It was an illogical thought, because she hadn't even been on one date with Levi —and she wasn't about to count tonight as a date, not after she'd kissed his brother. She picked up the orange bowling ball Simon had chosen for her and walked with Annie back to their lane in silence.

For the remainder of the game, Hannah simply went through the motions, too stunned by Simon's kiss and the effect it'd had on her to engage in much conversation. Levi had asked her several times if she was okay. She'd simply nodded and said she was tired from her long weekend and would need to cut the evening short—that when they'd finished their game, she'd need to leave.

As Levi stood to bowl his last set, Annie discreetly handed Hannah a piece of paper.

"What's this?" asked Hannah.

Annie lifted her face into a playful smile and gave her signature wink. "Either your history, or your future. That's up to you."

Hannah unfolded the paper. The beautiful rounded cursive read, "He finds her alone, secluded from others' eyes. He fights back his attraction, but his body aches with desire. The sky nods in approval as light beams shine down from the rising moon and illuminate her cheeks with its cool light. When she speaks of her desire for him and reaches for his chest, he knows that he will thirst only for her, now and forever. He kisses her gently at first, until she pulls him in with deeper desire. As he explores the deep reaches within her, her warm breath fills his chest with increased longing. The flame remains unquenched." *No kidding!* Hannah stopped reading to fan her face with the paper.

"Hannah, are you hot?" asked Levi as he tapped the top of the return ramp, waiting for his bowling ball to pop back out so he could complete the game with his last roll.

"Yep. You could say that," Hannah answered.

The second Levi had the bowling ball in his hands, Hannah continued reading. "Whisperings of eternal love encircle their intertwined souls. As the moonlight dissipates into the dark night, he reluctantly releases her, silently pleading for her to come to him again and make him whole."

Hannah closed her eyes and pressed her two fingertips to her lips. Annie thought Simon was hoping Hannah would make the next move. But how could she? Not only had he just walked away from her; he said he'd promised someone that he'd stay away from her. Why would someone make Simon promise to stay away from *her*? And if that was the case, why didn't they counsel Levi to do the same?

Hannah glanced up at Levi. He caught her eye and smiled. Everything about Levi was authentic and kind. The idea that she might hurt his feelings crushed her heart. She asked herself for the hundredth time that evening if "the talk" with him was necessary. Now that she had his friendship back after all of these years, she didn't want to let it go, which was perhaps why she'd allowed herself to lead him on. In the end, she agreed with Simon: it wasn't fair to Levi, and it needed to end.

"Great game, everyone!" Hannah announced, stuffing the paper under Annie's copy of *For Whom the Bell Tolls*. "It was so nice to have met you," she said to Annie and Paxton. "Levi, I need to go, but would you mind walking me out?"

Levi grabbed Hannah's hand before she had a chance to retrieve the piece of paper from under the book and slip it into her pocket.

She really wanted to have that note to remind her of how amazing the kiss with Simon had been—and to keep it away from inquiring eyes. At least it didn't contain their names or any physical characteristics that would give them away. She released a sigh of relief; no one would ever know Annie had written it about her and Simon.

As they stepped out into the crisp spring air, Levi draped his jacket around Hannah's shoulders. The moonlight reflected off the melting snow, lighting the mountain and creating a soft glow in the otherwise desolate night sky. "Hannah, I can't tell you how much comfort you've brought my family today ... and to me personally."

"Levi," she said, bowing her head and wrinkling her forehead. "I think I may have ..." She took in a deep breath. "I mean, I've really loved how we've been able to reestablish our friendship—a childhood friendship I'll always cherish."

His face dropped. "Friendship," he repeated in a deflated voice.

"Cherish forever," she said, reaching up and placing her hand on his shoulder when they reached her car. "But that's all I can offer you; it's all I'll ever be able to offer you. And I don't date co-workers." She removed his jacket from her shoulders and held it out to him.

He took a step back. "Keep it. Does this mean you're breaking up with me before we've started dating?"

Hannah's heart dropped. "When you put it that way ..." She searched for the words.

"You don't need to explain, Hannah. That was jerky of me, and I appreciate your honesty. I want us to be friends too."

She sighed out her relief. She thought she might have been too naïve to think that he'd settle for friendship, but it sounded like she'd been right. Simon had rejected her, but at least she still had Levi as a friend. "Great, because I can't tell you how happy I am to start hanging out with you again. I've missed those childhood days."

"Me too," he said with a forced smile. "Good night, Hannah." He kissed her cheek, ran to his car, and drove away.

She felt awful at rejecting him, but at least now she didn't need to worry about workplace romance. It was better this way—no more awkwardness at the office. Levi had liked her, but he was content with being friends. Simon didn't want to date her. She'd basically begged him to kiss her, and when he had, he'd stopped mid-kiss and said that was it for them. No matter. All would be back to normal tomorrow, as it had been before the Grant brothers. Her office and Simon's office were on different floors. They most likely would never see each other, and he would be off on his next international adventure before the summer was through. She thanked her lucky stars that Simon had no clue Annie had seen them kissing, then poetically penned the entire heart-pounding scene.

CHAPTER SEVEN

"*H*ere ya go, honey," said the coquettish young waitress, setting a basket of hot fries on the table in front of Simon. It wouldn't be Idaho without their signature starch and a side of fry sauce—the delectable dip made from ketchup, mayonnaise, and a hint of mustard.

"Thanks," said Simon, but he didn't look up at the waitress. His eyes remained glued on the bowling lane where Paxton had just brought Scout—Paxton and Annie's little three-year-old daughter. He threw a fry into his mouth, not realizing that it was still sizzling. He closed his mouth and moaned in pain.

Out of his peripheral vision, he noticed the waitress lift her nose and stomp away. She didn't seem pleased that he didn't appreciate her French fries, or maybe her anger had originated from his lack of interest in her. He'd never been much of a flirt—only with girls he really liked. But he'd also never been the reclusive, brooding type, not until today. He sat alone at the orange table in the dining area of the bowling alley and watched everyone else joke around.

Scout's corn silk curls bounced as she jumped up and

down. She giggled at the sound of the paper in her hands as she smashed it up into a ball. Simon wanted that piece of paper. He ran his fingers through his hair and twisted his lips. No, he *needed* that piece of paper, or he'd always wonder.

He hadn't taken his eyes off Hannah since he'd left her so abruptly after that amazing kiss they'd shared. He knew stalking her was wrong; that's why he hadn't followed her and Levi outside. Annie had slipped that paper to Hannah with a devious smile and a wink. He'd caught every second of their exchange. When Hannah had read whatever was on that piece of paper, she'd gotten so flustered that she'd closed her eyes and touched her lips.

He clenched his jaw, remembering how he'd seen Hannah and Levi holding hands while they walked out of the bowling alley a few minutes ago together. He, alone, had encouraged Hannah to get together with Levi, so he couldn't blame anyone but himself. He'd been an idiot. He'd had her in his arms less than an hour ago. Then he'd handed her over to Levi—more like he'd pushed her into Levi's arms.

"Uncle Simon has French fries!" shouted Scout, pointing at Simon.

Annie and Pax motioned for Scout to join Simon at his table. He loved being an adopted uncle. Paxton, Zee, and Kai Terrence had been like brothers to him growing up. The Terrences were a few years older and slightly less athletic than the Grant brothers, but the two families had gone on several vacations together. Some of Simon's favorite memories as a kid were sailing with the Terrences off the coast of San Francisco and zip-lining through the cloud forests of Costa Rica. He imagined splashing through the waves on a sailboat with Hannah—she would sport a black swimsuit, and the salty spray would cause her loose hair to glisten in the afternoon sunlight.

"Uncle Simon?" asked Scout, standing in front of him

with her head tilted so far to the side that if she leaned any farther, she'd tip over. "What are you looking at?"

He blinked a few times. "Only you, cutie. Want some fries?" he asked, standing to greet her. He lifted her up and placed her onto a chair across the table from him. "Dig in."

Her gigantic green eyes opened wide. They were a beautiful mix of Annie's hazel and Paxton's sea-foam green eyes. They resembled the new growth of the blue spruce evergreen trees in the spring—a light, fluorescent green. She wiggled her fingers in the air in anticipation for her snack, causing the ball of paper to drop to the table.

Simon's heart raced as he reached for the paper ball, but Scout got to it first. She picked it up, stuffed it inside her elbow, then brought her arm to her chest, locking it away from him.

She narrowed her eyes at him. "It's mine."

Simon sat back and rubbed his chin for a minute, then snapped his fingers. "You like things made out of paper?"

"Crinkly paper," she corrected him, biting into a fry dripping with fry sauce.

He nodded. "I understand. What if I gave you crinkly paper that can fly?"

She angled her face away from him but continued to watch him, as if she were interested but didn't want to seem so interested that she would lose her prized paper ball. She didn't answer him.

"Hold on." Simon ran to the restaurant counter and asked for a few sheets of the thin wax paper the restaurant used to wrap burgers and sandwiches in. The waitress who'd flirted with him earlier kindly handed him several sheets. He returned to the table to find half of his French fries gone. "I'm impressed," he said with a laugh. "Now, wait till you see this." He spent the next ten minutes folding the thin wax sheets into an assortment of airplanes and animal origami, from jumping frogs to flying cranes. Unfortunately, nothing seemed to get Scout to release her prized paper ball. He was running out of options—and paper. "Why don't you tell me what *you* want?" he said with an exhausted sigh, pushing the last sheet of wax paper toward her.

Her face lifted into an angelic smile. She took the paper from him and scrunched it up into a ball, laughing hysterically with every crunch of the crinkly wax paper, her eyes sparkling with mischief. She pushed the coveted paper ball across the table to him, then continued her paper party by smashing up the origami animals he'd folded.

Simon opened the white notebook paper he'd been mesmerized with for the past hour and smoothed it out onto the table with gusto. As his eyes scanned the elegant cursive, his insides heated to near sizzling—like that first French fry that had burned his mouth. Only this time it wasn't a small spot on the edge of his tongue that felt the burn. His entire body smoldered. "Ache with desire," the note read. Yep, that about summed it up. Simon reread the most poignant piece of the poem, "the flame that remains unquenched." He leaned back in the red vinyl diner chair and crossed his arms.

Annie bounced to the table, picked Scout up, and—to Scout's absolute delight—swung her around in the air. "Go see your daddy. He set up a bowling ramp for you."

"Yes!" shouted Scout before setting off at a run toward the bowling lanes.

Annie picked up a fry, dipped it in the salmon-colored fry sauce, and popped it into her mouth with a moan. "Why hasn't California caught on to fry sauce yet? They have no idea what they're missing."

Simon waved the paper in the air. "What's this, Annie?"

She ignored his question. "But you know what *you're*

missing," Annie stated with a wink. "Don't you, Simon? Tell me, do Hannah's kisses transport you to the moon?" She pointed to him with her French fry before dipping it. "Do her kisses make you feel like you're standing on a Grecian beach or on the precipice of a mountain?" She swirled her fry in the sauce and stared into space, as if her mind had just taken *her* somewhere enchanting.

"What do you know that I don't?" Simon sat back in his chair and rubbed his chin. "You got all chummy with Hannah. Why don't we start there?"

Annie placed her black purse next to the fries, grabbed out a handful of candies, and tossed them onto the table.

Simon's mouth watered. "Are those your signature caramels? The ones you wrote about in your last 'How to' book? What was it titled again … *How to Train Your Husband?*"

"*How to Train a Husband,*" she corrected him. "It's a romantic comedy about using doggie training techniques to train a man to be the perfect companion." She wrinkled her nose—something she did when she was irritated with something, or someone. "You're thinking *How to Train Your Husband,* because someone put out a low-budget movie the year after my book released with that title."

"That's right!" Simon said with a laugh. "I'd heard that from Pax a while back and told him I know a few amazing copyright attorneys who you can chat with. I remember him saying that when he'd watched the movie, he was amazed at how similar the main character was to yours. Sounds like you have grounds for an infringement lawsuit."

"There were several similarities between my book and the movie, but that's not my style." She waved a hand in the air. "I should be flattered, but I'm not. I might have been if I'd enjoyed the movie more."

"You know what I plan on enjoying?" he asked, picking up

a caramel. "These yummy treats. Do I need to beg for it?" he joked.

"Actually," she said with raised a brow, "I was thinking quid pro quo. Treat for information. You need to tell me if I described that kiss accurately." She tapped her finger on the paper.

He'd been waiting for her to bring up why she'd written those lines and what her conversation with Hannah had been. He stared into Annie's hazel eyes, wondering how much to divulge. After all, Hannah might choose Levi. This conversation could come back to haunt him someday. "This would be a lot easier if I knew that Hannah had told you she enjoyed that kiss."

"If I'm sharing, I get a treat." Annie slowly unwrapped a caramel and popped it in her mouth. "Don't quote me on this, but she's drawn to you like a firefly to sweet nectar."

He tilted his chin down and shot her an eye of disbelief. "Then why did she leave with Levi?"

"Who was the one who stopped the *amazing* kissing scene short, again?" Annie didn't flinch. "And who said she left with Levi?"

Hope filled his chest as he leaned forward. "She didn't leave with Levi?" he asked with a wide grin.

"Oh, come on," Annie said impatiently, handing him a caramel. "Your turn."

He took the candy from her. "Okay. You were spot-on."

"Yes!" she said with glee. "I haven't lost my touch. These little ego boosts do more for my creative juices than you could ever imagine."

He laughed. "Glad I could help. Now, what can you tell me about Hannah?"

"We're leaving tomorrow afternoon, but I thought I'd invite her to lunch. I'll have more for you tomorrow. Just one word of advice."

"You're gonna tell me whether I want to hear it or not."

"Good boy." She winked and patted his cheek. "Be yourself. My guess is she longs for the adventure and intensity that a life with you would bring."

"Why do I feel like a dog right now with you patting my cheek? You still researching for that book?"

"No," she said with a smile. "But I'll never be finished with helping people fall in love; it's the grandest thing in the world." She pointed at him. "Don't repeat this, but something I learned the hard way from my research on training up the perfect husband was that a puppy's bad behavior originates with their owner." She turned her pointer finger toward herself. "In the end, I was the one who got trained."

Simon scratched his chin. "So it's Paxton I should be talking to."

Annie whistled. "Yes, but not to learn how to train." She glanced over at Paxton. "My Navy SEAL husband could show you a thing or two on how to be a *real* man." She waggled her eyebrows.

"I don't doubt that." Simon slapped his thighs and laughed. "So, Hannah wants a tough guy?"

"My guess is she wants a guy who'll take a fist to the eye to protect her. You don't get much tougher than that, Simon. Like I said, be yourself."

He lightly touched the sore area beneath his eye. He'd almost forgotten about that altercation. "Hannah thinks I'm tough?"

Annie leaned forward, placing her elbows onto the table and resting her chin into her woven fingers. "Only one way to find out. You in?"

He plucked Annie's pen out of her messy bun. "Where do I sign?" he asked.

"This is gonna be so fun," she squealed. "And I already

have a few great ideas on how to make her fall in love with you."

In love with me? If Annie really thought that a possibility, then he needed to up his game. "Matchmaker Annie, it's time to make me a match."

CHAPTER EIGHT

*T*he midday sunlight warmed Hannah's cheeks. "Well, hello there!" she said to the friendly blue jay who'd followed her from the parking lot and perched himself under the gable of Sun Valley Grill. She'd recommended the upscale grill to Annie because of the stunning views and buttery steak hamburgers. Annie had mentioned during their chat at the bowling alley last night that she'd grown up on a dairy farm in Wisconsin and craved corn-fed beef, a delicacy bordering on illegal in northern Cali where she lived. When Hannah told Annie about the Grill, Annie had insisted that she join the rest of the Terrence women for lunch before their flights out of town.

Hannah stepped into the upscale pub—more bar than restaurant—to the aroma of grilled steak and freshly baked bread. If Annie and her girlfriends were looking for a light meal, they were out of luck today.

Mylie, the current manager of Sun Valley Grill and an old childhood friend of Hannah's, walked up to her with a wide grin. "Hey there, stranger! Back patio?" she asked, giving Hannah a quick hug.

"It's open?" asked Hannah as she followed Mylie through the restaurant. "But there's still snow on the ground."

Mylie cocked an eyebrow. "There's no snow on our *heated* patio. We only service those individuals who really want the posh, *elevated* experience," she said with a competitive smile, dissing the Mandolin. "Say the word, Hannah. I'd love to have you come work here with me."

Hannah enjoyed her friend's spunk. "You're sweet, but I'll be dropping my shifts at the Mandolin as soon as I can get them covered. I've taken a position with Grant and Grant," she said, stepping outside onto the back patio. Mylie had been good to her word; the patio was warmer than inside the restaurant, with all six of the tall outdoor propane heaters burning. Hannah walked to the edge of the patio and admired the unobstructed view of the mountain: a small stream and a horse pasture, white with snow, separated the Grill from the cotton-wrapped mountain. A smile crossed Hannah's lips; she loved slack season and the quiet of the town—and her mountain—for those glorious few weeks before the summer season hit.

"I'm really happy for you, Hannah. It sounds like life is treating you good. I'll watch out for the rest of your party and make sure you girls get your privacy." Mylie walked away before Hannah had a chance to thank her.

The patio held ten small tables, but it sounded like they'd have the area to themselves since Mylie wasn't planning on seating anyone else outside with Hannah's party. She placed her purse on the table closest to the metal railing and focused on the amazing view by leaning against the black iron fence that prevented the pub's guests from slipping down into the babbling brook, twenty feet underfoot. With the snowpack beginning its spring melt, the stream had swelled two or three feet wide, at least by Hannah's quick estimation. She closed her eyes and listened intently to the frigid mountain water as it gurgled over the rocks and splashed against the tree roots that extended out from the riverbank and into the water's path. As she concentrated on the calming sounds of nature, her shoulders naturally dropped, and her breathing slowed with complete relaxation.

The trees at Hannah's side rustled moments before an obnoxious squawk disrupted her reverie. Her eyes shot open and she glared at the pesky blue jay now perched on the railing next to her. "You should never say hello to certain men." She shook her finger at the bird. "And you, my friend, are one of those men. You are loud, irreverent, and ridiculously rude."

The blue jay crowed louder, causing Hannah to throw her head back and laugh.

"Hannah?" said Annie.

Hannah turned and smiled at Annie and the three women she'd brought. They were all close to her age, maybe a few years older.

Annie winked at her friends. "I told you she's a modern-day Snow White. When she speaks, the birds answer. Hannah, this is Meri, Tori, and Ariana."

The tallest, and quite possibly the most beautiful woman Hannah had ever met, stepped forward and gave Hannah a firm embrace, leaving her slightly breathless due to both the woman's beauty and her strong hug. "I'm Meri, Kai and Zee's sister, and Paxton's cousin, who I believe you bowled with last night. Annie told us all about you this morning."

Annie continued, "This is Tori and Ariana. Tori is married to Zee, and Ariana is married to Kai."

Tori stood almost as tall as Meri, with long, silky brown hair and hazel eyes. Ariana had a more unique look, with deep auburn red hair and vibrant green eyes that had a gentle shyness about them.

"Thanks for letting me join you for your girls' lunch," said Hannah.

Their waiter stepped outside to take their drink order, interrupting their greeting with a pleasant nod. The waiter's presence reminded Hannah that she needed to get back to the law office before too long; she didn't want anyone at the law firm to think she was a slacker who took two-hour lunch breaks every day.

Hannah said, "When did you guys say you needed to fly out? Because I can recommend some items from the menu that are quick and delicious."

Meri stepped closer. "It's nice to see someone other than myself taking charge. Great idea. Let's get our orders into the kitchen. Hannah, suggest away."

The waiter seemed a little peeved to be rushed and that he didn't have the opportunity to tell them the restaurant's daily specials or provide any input, but he handled it relatively well—giving only one scowl that quickly transformed into a courtesy smile. He wrote their orders with an efficient scratch of his pen on his notepad, nodded, then left them.

Once they'd settled into their seats, Annie pulled a pack of white index cards out of her purse and placed them onto the table. "I have a fun activity for us."

"Annie, what are you up to?" asked Tori with a sideways glance. "You have that mischievous sparkle in your eyes again, like you did when you set me up with Zee."

Annie raised both eyebrows, opened her eyes wide, and innocently shook her head. "I have no idea what you're talking about."

Meri folded her arms across her chest. "I'm not buying it either. Something smells amuck here."

Annie tsked her tongue. "Nothing smells amuck. I just wanted to run some ideas by you for a new book or two. You know the *How to Train a Husband* book? Well … I'm throwing down some ideas and researching the concept of *How to Complete a Bucket List by Age 40,* or *How to Conquer All Your Fears in Less than a Year.*" Annie opened her pack of lined note cards and wrote one of those goals on the top of each card.

"Oh, I love it," Ariana, the redhead, chimed in. "I've got one: *How to Be Green with Our Aquamarine.*"

Tori leaned into Hannah's ear and said, "Ari's a bio-conservationist working to save tree frogs in Costa Rica."

Hannah nodded in understanding. "Is this kind of like *How to Lose a Boyfriend,* where the girl takes her guy to a Carla Dean concert in Vegas to get him to want to break up with her?"

"Exactly," said Annie, snapping her fingers. She wrote *Carla Dean in concert* at the top of one of the cards. "Here are a few cards." She quickly scribbled either *Bucket List* or *Fears* on the cards and tossed them around to everyone.

Hannah grabbed the card with *Carla Dean in concert* written at the top and waved it in the air. "That'll be on my list for sure," she said with a straight face, laughing inside—not that Carla wasn't an amazing singer; Hannah just couldn't imagine a concert at the top of any bucket list. "I'm going to write *all* my fears on this one."

No one seemed to pay much attention to her or laugh at her joke. They were all too busy coming up with their own fears and dreams.

"Hannah, here's a pen," said Annie, handing Hannah a red sparkly pen with a fuzzy tuft on top like a cartoon character.

"It's … beautiful," Hannah stuttered out.

Meri glanced up from her cards just long enough to shoot Annie a questioning look. Annie smiled back at Meri innocently. Meri tilted her head back down to her cards with an amused expression tugging at her lips. Hannah had known girls in high school who got pleasure out of teasing other girls; they'd toyed with them as if they were their pets. Hannah really hoped she wasn't the pet here, because she liked these girls and hoped the relationships would continue. Only time would tell.

Hannah focused on Annie's request. She considered what she wanted to do before she kicked the bucket and the things that scared her the most. She would start with her fears and end with happy, hopeful thoughts to put on her bucket list. She shuddered with the image of a shark attacking her in the ocean. She wrote, *No. 1: Snorkel with large, dangerous marine life in the ocean*.

Everyone was still staring off into the distance and writing their thoughts when the waiter brought their food outside. It was unlike any girls' gathering Hannah had ever had. Most friend luncheons involved lots and lots of talking and laughing, but she wasn't complaining; this way she could enjoy the sounds of nature *and* be with new friends.

The next vision that came to her mind was a memory that paralyzed her with fear every time she sat in the passenger seat of a car that wound along a mountainous road. She'd been in an accident as a child where the car had slid off the road and down the side of a cliff before colliding with a tree. The smell of the broken branches and gas fumes were as vivid in her mind as they were the night it happened. She wrote, *No. 2: Be a passenger in a car driving fast on a winding road*.

Hannah took a big bite of her burger. The savory juices dripped down her chin. Luckily, no one else caught her sloppiness before she wiped it with her cloth napkin. As she touched the napkin to her chin, she recalled being struck in the face with a pop-up ball during a softball game as a kid. Ever since that fateful game, she'd never played any sports with small balls shooting at her—like tennis or racquetball. *No. 3: Play a sport where small flying balls shoot at me*.

Hannah's heart couldn't take much more trauma. "How many do we need on each card, Annie?"

Annie shrugged. "Four … or five." Then she took another bite of her hamburger. "Hannah, these burgers are to die for."

"I think if we ate these every day, we would die," said Ariana with a scratch to the side of her head.

Annie sighed. "She's an environmentalist."

"You say that like it's a bad thing," Ariana huffed out. She smiled. "But I'm used to it. You should hear the grief that Kai gives me."

"Didn't he try to get you to eat a snake last year that the Grant twins had killed in Florida and made into jerky?" said Meri with a laugh.

"That was *not* funny," Ariana responded, trying to keep a straight face. "They told me it was beef jerky—like that's not bad enough."

The entire table erupted into laughter.

"Thanks for helping me with my last one." Hannah set her hamburger down and wrote, *No. 4: Wrestle a large snake who wants to eat me.* Perhaps writing down her fears was like knocking on wood, and it would prevent her from ever having to experience them. Now she just needed to come up with a few things for her bucket list. She handed her *Fear* card to Annie and grabbed another index card from the center of the table. "This has been such a fun way to spend lunch. Thanks for inviting me," Hannah told everyone. "I'd love to hear the results."

"Oh, you will," Annie said with increased enthusiasm. "I'd bet a billionaire on that one."

∼

*S*imon leaned against the metal siding of the private hangar. The loud buzz of airplane engines didn't help settle his nerves. Annie had sounded more distressed on the phone than he'd ever known her to be, muttering something about having to see him before she boarded the plane.

What had her so upset that she'd call and beg me to leave the office that minute to meet her at the airport? If Pax messed up, I'm gonna kill him myself! Simon's mind, at times, skipped reason in favor of absolute irrationality. He rubbed his chin, hoping his mind had simply concocted the worst-case scenario.

"Simon!" yelled Annie in a cheery voice as she bounced out of the main receiving hangar, followed by the rest of the Terrences. "Thanks for coming so quickly. This is going to make it all worth it." She handed him an index card with handwritten notes.

He scratched his eyebrow while he took the paper from her. "*This* is what I came down here for?"

"That," she said, tapping on the paper, "is Hannah's bucket list. You can thank me now, or later."

Simon sighed. "Bucket list? Annie, are you always this cryptic?"

"Yes," said Zee with a laugh, walking up behind them. "And she's the most annoying kid sister you'll ever meet."

"I'm starting to see that," Simon said with a raised brow.

"Are you kidding me?" yelled Annie to Zee as he passed them on his way to their jet. "I'm the reason you and Tori got together, or maybe got back together, or stayed together. Whatever I did, it worked, and it'll work for Simon as well," she said with a confident nod.

Simon read the first line on the card. "Carla Dean? She seriously wants to go to that girly concert before she dies?"

Annie shrugged. "What's wrong with that? Carla's one of

73

the best vocalists in the world. Why wouldn't Annie want to go? And other than the one concert wish, her desires border on adrenaline-junkie wild. You've got yourself an adventurous woman there. She's almost as daring as you, Simon. I think you two crazies are perfect for each other."

Simon scratched his neck as he continued down the list, then looked back up at Annie. "You're telling me she wants to wrestle a snake ... that wants to *eat* her?" He narrowed his eyes. "Are you sure about this, Annie?"

"She's the one who wrote it," she said, throwing her arms down at her sides.

Simon's chest nearly burst with excitement at the prospect of Hannah being so daring. "But it doesn't say 'bucket list' anywhere on this card."

"I'm confident this is what she wants," Annie said with resolution. "She said Carla Dean would be on her list for sure. Then she kept on writing." She gave Simon a kiss on his cheek. "By the end of the summer, you'll have made all her dreams come true."

"You think we'll be married by the end of the summer?" Simon asked. "I'm good, but maybe not that good."

Annie waggled her eyebrows. "That's all it took for Ariana and Kai. Right, Ari?" she yelled over her shoulder. "Weren't you married only a few months after you first met Kai?"

"Yes," answered Kai, smacking Simon's shoulder. "But now she blames our whirlwind romance on a brain hemorrhage."

"I do not!" Ari yelled while walking up the stairs to the jet. "I blame it on your sexy eyes and your beguiling smell."

"Beguiling smell?" Simon laughed, pretending to sniff his friend. "Would you want to take your sailboat out if Hannah and I jet down to Costa Rica?"

Kai opened his arms and chest in a welcoming gesture.

"Anytime. You know that's why Ariana fell for me, right? Because I taught her how to sail. That's all it'll take, man."

They spent the next few minutes saying their goodbyes, and then the Terrences boarded their jet and were in the air in less than twenty minutes. Simon set off at a sprint for his car with plans churning through his mind on how to make Hannah's every dream come true.

CHAPTER NINE

*a*t 6:29 a.m., the sun's first rays burst over the snowy mountain, driving away the darkness with its ethereal light.

"Beautiful morning." Hannah sighed out her gratitude as she stared out her office window and sipped her morning tea. She had so much to be grateful for. She'd found her dream job right out of law school; not many attorneys could say that.

The past few weeks working at Grant and Grant had been exceptional, and things had settled with Levi and Simon. They went to lunch often together, but the conversations were light. The flirtatious glances and winking had stopped. Although she did catch Simon staring at her from time to time, which caused her to blush as she relieved their kiss. She'd thought about texting Annie to ask her what had happed to the kissing note, so she could relive the moment that would, as Annie had said, be part of her history. She sighed. It would always be a beautiful and thrilling part of her history, but unfortunately, that's all it could ever be, because Simon had turned out to be a thrill-seeking playboy.

Not that he talked about other women when she was around, but all anyone had to do was look at Simon and know to be careful.

"Hannah, can you come into my office, please?" Mr. Grant's voice emanated through Hannah's desk phone.

"Yes, sir. I'll be in your office momentarily." She walked the few yards to her boss's office and knocked on the open thick wooden door. He never seemed to shut his door, lending a comfortable, inviting ambience to the firm.

"Come in, Hannah," he said in his deep, commanding voice. "How's your month at Grant and Grant been?"

She took a seat at the table and clasped her hands together. "Wonderful. I never thought I'd work with humanitarian efforts, and it's been both challenging and rewarding."

"I admire your tenacity," he said, scratching his cheek as he took his seat across from her. "You're the only other person driven enough be in the office by six a.m., then willing to stay for a solid twelve hours. I'm glad I've placed you in our charitable division. My wife suggested that one, and she was right, as always. I've decided to extend your scope. You'll not only be managing and coordinating our philanthropic outreach here in the continental US, but also in several foreign countries. It's quite something to see how a little time and a generous amount of resources can change the lives of people living in the extreme poverty."

Hannah clapped her hands. "Put me to work, sir."

Mr. Grant sat back and laughed. "And that's why I hired you. I'm sending you and Simon down to Las Vegas this morning to meet with an associate of ours from Africa. I've already had my assistant book your rooms and front-row tickets to the show in that hotel this evening."

Hannah gasped as heat rose in her cheeks. *Las Vegas with Simon!* She covered her gaping mouth with her hand and forced down the lump in her throat. "You'd like me to fly down to Las Vegas and spend the weekend there with Simon?"

"Actually, you'll be driving down together. There weren't any flights to Las Vegas today, and I need you two there before 6:00 p.m. Our associate is flying out of Vegas this evening for Africa."

She turned her wrist to examine her watch. "If we left right now and didn't stop, we'd get there at, what ... 4:30? Is it even possible to make that appointment?"

"They're an hour earlier. You'll be fine. But I told Simon he needs to pick you up by 7:00. Will that work for you?"

Hannah nodded. "I'll run home now and pack."

Mr. Grant smiled. "That's what I thought. You and Simon are going to make a fine team. Just wait and see."

Hannah rubbed her lips together to keep from saying something stupid, then hurried out of his office.

~

Simon's tires crunched as he pulled up Hannah's gravel driveway. Her home was one of the more rustic cabin-styled homes that were off the beaten path, but everything in Ketchum, Idaho, was off the beaten path.

Levi hadn't been happy when he'd heard Simon was taking Hannah down to Las Vegas, but he hadn't gotten as bent out of shape as he normally did—which put Simon on his guard, because Levi could very well be planning a coup. Levi was entirely capable of staging a takeover. With Annie's encouragement, Simon had a plan to win Hannah's heart, but it would need to be a slow process. He didn't want his actions to catch Levi's eye. As things stood, Levi didn't know how intoxicated and transfixed Simon had become with

Hannah, and Simon needed to keep it that way for the time being.

He hopped out of his car just as Hannah emerged from her house. His heart nearly stopped as he watched her glide toward him. Even in the early morning light, her natural beauty radiated. "Good morning, Hannah. You look amazing."

She tossed her carry-on bag into his open trunk and glared at him. "Let's get something straight. Just because we're going to Las Vegas together doesn't mean I'm a flavor of the week. We're never kissing again. Ever. Our relationship is business. Period." Dang, she was cute when she was mad. She obviously wasn't happy about how he'd walked away from their kiss.

"So, mornings aren't really your thing," he said, opening her car door for her.

She looked away from him, as if hiding a smile, and wiggled into the passenger's seat. "Not today."

"You know," he said, settling into the driver's seat, "the only thing to chase away the morning blues is to listen to some pick-me-up blues."

Now Hannah *did* smile at him. "How did you know that I like blues that's upbeat?"

"A little bird told me," he said, pulling out onto the road. "A beautiful little bird named Hannah."

She narrowed her eyes at him. "I did not."

Simon tapped the button on his steering wheel and said, "Play Hannah's playlist." He glanced at her as the ragtime music began. "Yes. You did. You also thought I was slow that night."

She tossed her head back and laughed. "Still to be determined."

"We have a ten-hour drive ahead of us. Do you think that's long enough for you to determine my IQ?"

"Hardly," she said with a playful smile he wished he could pay more attention to, but he couldn't—he was the one driving.

"Let me know if you want to drive." *So I can stare at you.*

"You wouldn't mind a woman driving?" she asked in an accusatory way.

He could play along with this banter. "Hey, if you like it when a man takes the clutch, I have no problem with that."

Her nose twitched. "Pull over," she instructed.

He pulled to the side of the road a few hundred feet before their on-ramp. "Your call," he said with an internal smile, patting himself on the back. He could stare at her all day now. He sat in the driver's seat and struck up a conversation. "Want a bottle of water?"

"No thanks. Long drive. I don't want to have to stop that often or we won't make dinner with our African associate, and I want to have lots of room for the award-winning buffet."

They'd always kept their conversations superficial. It was time to dig deeper, let her know he was really interested in her story. "So, where have you been all these years?"

"Me?" She pointed to herself. "Where have *I* been? For starters, I've been home every holiday. Where have you been?"

"Touché. But I'm not here to argue with you, Hannah. I'm sorry about that kiss. It must have been horrible."

Her face flushed and she bit at her bottom lip, looking straight ahead at the road.

Whatever he'd said, it had made her uncomfortable, but it brought a gorgeous shade of pink to her face. "Truce?" he asked. "I'll try to behave myself. And …" He held up a finger. "I'll even go first and tell you something that you don't know about me, like how a swarm of honeybees in Spain chased me into a lake."

"Honeybees don't chase people," she said defiantly.

"You wanna bet?" he replied. He told her about his adventures in Spain, England, France, and then Greece. She smiled a lot, which told him that maybe he had a chance. As the hours passed, it seemed as if Hannah was lowering her guard, opening herself up more and more, which intensified his need to protect her from the outside world—and by outside world, he meant men, which also created in him more guilt. If he dated Hannah, it would crush Levi, but if he couldn't be with Hannah, then it would shatter him. He recommitted himself to not trying to get Hannah to fall for him, but he couldn't quit entirely because he'd started on the bucket list project. All the flights had been purchased, and every activity scheduled and paid for.

"So, you're a wanderer? Searching for something." She pointed at him. "Let me ask you this: have you found what you've been searching for, or are you headed out on another world tour?"

"I've been traveling the world in search of ..." As he spoke, he received a moment of clarity and inspiration so distinct that it was almost as if his mind shouted *You*! Good thing he hadn't said it out loud, or she might have turned the car around.

"Searching for what?" she asked with intrigue.

"For the meaning of life."

"And did you find it?"

Simon focused on how the vein in her neck pulsated. He swallowed down the glowing desire in his chest to press his lips to the throbbing vein. He rubbed his chin. "Yeah. Yeah, I did."

"And what *is* the meaning of life?"

"I'm guessing it's different for everyone."

She shook her head, irritated. "You're not answering my question."

"Don't worry. I'll tell you someday, but only after you discover the meaning of life for yourself … perhaps through experiencing things you've always dreamed of doing."

"Wouldn't that be nice," she said with a sigh. "But we don't all have millions of dollars to throw at our dreams." She held up a hand as if in apology. "Not that I'm coveting yours. I'm happy for you. So, that's how you found the answers, by traveling the world?"

"Yes," he drew out. "But not in the way you think."

"Since I'm not getting anywhere with this topic, tell me about Africa."

With the mere mention of Africa, Simon could already feel her hand in his as they walked along the dusty paths. "You're going to love it there! Acachi, the guy we're meeting with tonight, is a good friend, translator, guide, and geologist who tells us where to dig the wells."

"I'm going to Africa?" Hannah asked with the excitement of a child tasting whipped cream for the first time.

Simon laughed. "Of course."

"I've always wanted to go on a safari and see the wildlife up close. I've been thinking about that since around the time I started at Grant and Grant."

"I'll also take you to Guatemala, Panama, Columbia, the Congo, and many more exotic and wonderful places."

"Together?" Her brows knitted with concern. "Like you and me?" The faint blush returned to her cheeks.

"Unless, of course, you're worried about falling in love with me."

"Cocky much?" she asked, turning her attention back to the road.

"You're a great driver. I feel so relaxed when you drive that I may even doze off—but just to warn you, I sometimes sleep with my eyes open, so don't worry if it looks like I'm staring."

Her forehead wrinkled. "That's weird."

"No. It's normal."

"No. It's not," she said with a sideways glance.

The buzz of Hannah's phone interrupted their banter.

"Will you check that text?" she asked. "It could be the office."

"Sure," he said, holding the phone out to her for her fingerprint.

Simon read the text from Levi aloud: "Hannah, rainbow trout are jumping. Want to go fly fishing on Sunday in Silver Creek? Friends fish together."

Slimy little devil, thought Simon, but then he repented with a remorseful heart. He just couldn't seem to help falling for Hannah, and he wanted Hannah to fall for him.

Hannah cleared her throat. "I'll text him back when we stop."

Simon glanced at the gas gauge. "We probably won't want to stop until we hit Salt Lake City for gas, or we may be too pressed for time." If she didn't respond for a solid three hours to Levi, then he and Levi would both know that she wasn't interested in Levi. The heat was on; he'd need to find a way to impress her. "This drive reminds me of the time I drove the wrong way in an English countryside," he laughed. "Those farmers sure hated me."

"Now that sounds like an adventure," she said with a blink of her green eyes.

CHAPTER TEN

The theater swelled with crackling energy and expensive perfume as every seat filled. Hannah glanced around the room, admiring the thousands of red velvet seats where gold sparkling gowns and black suits swept up and down the aisles. Carla Dean was known for her gold gowns, which her fans mimicked, but Hannah preferred her simple black dress. She certainly wasn't alone in wearing her little black dress, but she was one of the few people there who didn't wear their money on their sleeve, literally.

"Hannah, I got us some T-shirts." Simon returned to their seats holding up a large black T-shirt with gold lettering that said *I Brake for Carla Dean* on the front and *Kiss to Make Up*—Carla's most popular love song—on the back. "I told the salesperson that we were sitting on the front row, and he said that when the security guys run down the aisles, that's when we should throw these on and sprint to the stage."

Sprint! Hannah thought. She wouldn't be sprinting anywhere, not since she'd stuffed herself at the buffet. She hadn't even noticed how much she was eating; she'd gotten wrapped up in the intriguing conversation with their associate from Africa. She was mesmerized by his report of what the Grant Foundation had already achieved and what they were gearing up to do. "After that amazing buffet, I'm not sure I'll be sprinting anywhere, even the five feet to the stage. You might have to roll me," she said, clutching her stomach. And she wasn't lying: she'd stuffed herself silly with everything from freshly boiled snow crab to prime rib to mini cheesecakes dusted with saffron.

Her comment had its desired effect; Simon laughed, which filled her with happiness. During the ten-hour drive down, she'd learned to not only love his laugh, but to crave it. It made her giddy just listening to him chuckle. The first thirty minutes of their drive had been awkward, but she'd eventually relaxed into an easy rhythm of conversation. They'd chatted the entire drive without those uncomfortable silences that happened when two people barely knew each other but were forced into a confined space together. In fact, Hannah had to keep reminding herself that this wasn't a date with Simon; this was business. And if it wasn't business, it would just be a weekend fling for the playboy. He'd probably left a girlfriend in every city he'd traveled to. She needed to keep her heart in check.

"Thanks for the T-shirt. It's very … sparkly."

He laughed again. "Don't take any photos of me in this, and I'll let you live."

She punched him in the arm. "You're the one who bought them."

"I just want this evening, and show, to be perfect for you, Hannah. I hope that it's everything you've imagined."

She tilted her head to the side and stared at him, not understanding if he was trying to seduce her or let her know how weird he thought she was.

"Why are you looking at me like that?" he laughed out.

She bit her lower lip to prevent herself from speaking.

"Come on," he encouraged her.

"It's just …" She sighed and pointed to the back of the T-shirt, where it said *Kiss to Make Up.* "I'm just wondering how many girls around the world are waiting, and hoping, you'll walk in their door tonight."

"Hopefully only one," he said as the lights dimmed and the red velvet curtains opened to a full orchestra.

Hannah didn't look over at the stage; her eyes remained transfixed on the man next to her.

~

*S*imon's neck ached. Whoever said that front-row tickets were the best had never been on the front row before. Even though he measured 6'3," he still had to tip his head back to get a good view of the stage.

This stage wasn't particularly extraordinary. The orchestra was set up along the right side of the stage, the backup signers of the left and the piano in the center under a huge chandelier where Carla Dean stood. The level of entertainment was on par with the other shows he'd seen in Las Vegas and New York City, but this show was unique because Simon had someone who loved it to share it with.

The show only had a few minutes remaining, but poor Hannah had stood on her tippy toes for most of it, although she didn't seem to mind. She hadn't sung every word to every song, like the rest of the crazy fans around them had, but she swayed to the music and smiled—smiled up at *him*. His chest nearly burst open every time she smiled over at him with that tantalizing mouth of hers. He'd dreamt about her lips since the night they'd kissed, and now her lips were so close, and she seemed like she'd accept his kiss if he offered it, but he couldn't. And he absolutely shouldn't.

When a flash of black ran past them down the aisle,

Hannah tapped Simon's arm, signaling the last song and their cue to sprint to the stage. He nodded, throwing on the shirt. She'd slipped her T-shirt on and grabbed his hand to pull him to the stage while he still wrestled to get his shirt even at the hem. When they'd reached the stage, he motioned for her to stand in front of him. He firmed his arms around her sides and pressed his palms into the stage to keep anyone from bumping into her. Luckily, the guards nodded to him and stood next to Hannah with their backs to the stage, instead of asking Hannah to stand farther away. The space around them filled quickly as Carla Dean retook the stage in a shimmering gold, slinky backless dress.

The crowd went nuts when she started singing "Kiss to Make Up." Simon had heard it a hundred times on the radio, but he couldn't deny how amazing it sounded live with a full orchestra accompanying her vocals.

Simon's body tensed as the back of a callused hand slid down the underside of his arm from behind. He looked down just as the hand grabbed hold of Hannah's breast. Simon shot his elbow back as he turned, nailing the guy in his nose and sending him flying backward into a stocky woman.

Hannah crisscrossed her arms over her chest and glared at Simon. With narrowed eyes and pursed lips, she slapped his face before he had a chance to explain. Carla Dean waved a hand in the air and the music cut. The bouncers were on Hannah's assailant within seconds, causing Hannah to shake her head in apology, grab the front of Simon's shirt, and mouth something about being sorry to his wide eyes, which were now watering from her slap. Man, she knew how to slap a guy into a stunned state.

Carla Dean walked to the front of the stage as the bouncers wrestled the attacker out of the auditorium. "What

I just witnessed in my concert is worthy of jail time, and I promise you, that man will get it."

The audience erupted into deafening applause.

Carla continued. "I need to apologize to these fine people," she said, looking at Simon and Hannah. "What are your names?"

Hannah answered, "This is Simon, and I'm Hannah."

"Well, Hannah and Simon, I want to apologize for what happened just now and for the misunderstanding that followed." She turned her attention back to the audience. "Did everyone see on our monitors what happened?" she asked, pointing to the screens on either side of the theater. The crowd shouted affirmatively. "I love all of you so much, especially Simon and Hannah for coming here tonight to spend the evening with me, and I would like to dedicate this next song to them. Because after what just happened, there's a lot of making up to do." She reached down and held Hannah's and Simon's hands. "Now, for this song to be effective, you must kiss during the entire song." She released their hands and returned to the center of the stage.

"Hannah, we don't have to—" said Simon, but before he could finish his sentence, Hannah pulled him down by the neck and kissed him.

That small act was all it took for Simon's entire body to explode. He returned her kiss with all the passion she'd unleashed in him.

Carla Dean took a bow, then began singing her kissing song for a second time. The audience cheered louder than they had all evening. Simon wasn't sure if the audience clapped for his and Hannah's kiss or for Carla Dean singing her signature song again. It didn't matter. Either way, he wouldn't forget this moment for the rest of his life. He'd always remember how their lips vibrated in unison to the sultry music, how she tasted like salted caramel, and how he never wanted to stop.

Hannah kissed him with a deeper longing than she had that first time at the bowling alley, causing him to cave. He knew in that moment that he'd do anything she asked. His head was crazy gone for her, and he knew he'd fight forever to stay this powerless. The question remained: should he tell her, or keep his feelings hidden from her until things were settled with Levi? He shot-putted Levi from his mind as quickly as his brother had entered and continued connecting with Hannah, focusing on expressing his affection in one of the oldest forms known to man, the delicate yet thrilling touch of forgiveness: the makeup kiss.

~

*H*annah flipped onto her side and beat her pillow with her fist to make it more comfortable, although she knew the act of beating her pillow wouldn't help her sleep better. Thoughts of Simon were what kept her awake, not her bed sheets, but hitting her pillow released the mounting frustration of not being in Simon's arms.

She grabbed her phone from off the hotel's nightstand and Googled Simon Grant. She sat up in bed, clutching her phone tight when she saw what was trending. She smacked her forehead with her palm. *Idiot!* she yelled at herself. How had anyone picked him out of that crowd? She scrunched her face and closed one eye with embarrassment while she watched the video. The recording began on the second note of "Kiss to Make Up," with the camera lens focused on the huge screen mounted on the side wall of the theater. Hannah moaned out her embarrassment and crossed her arms over her chest when the video showed the perp grabbing hold of her breast.

She wanted to catapult her phone across the room, but then the video showed Simon shoving the guy out of the way. She chuckled as the perp flew back from Simon's blow. It was unfortunate that a few other audience members had broken his fall. That had been the second time in a month that a hideous man had assaulted her, and Simon had been there to help. And those were the only times in her life she'd ever been grabbed like that. The odds seemed slim that Simon would be present for both.

In the clip, it was obvious that Simon wasn't the guy who'd grabbed her, but to her mortification, she'd been caught on film giving him an angry glare, then smacking him silly. She pinched the bridge of her nose and bowed her head, wondering how many people had seen the video—she couldn't bring herself to look. She didn't have Annie's note anymore, but at least she could keep this video to remind her of the amazing second kiss she and Simon had shared.

As if on cue, the video showed her pulling Simon down and kissing him. Yep, the kiss had been initiated one hundred percent by her this time. At least he'd returned her kiss and waited until the song had ended to stop kissing her, but any man would have in front of a live audience. It was the thirty minutes after the kiss that was telling. Simon had received a text on his phone before they'd left the theater. The text seemed to irritate him; perhaps it had been from the person that disapproved of their relationship.

Following the concert, Simon had walked Hannah back to her room, then said good night as if they'd just had a business meeting, not exchanged a timeless kiss in front of thousands of people, and now hundreds of thousands, according to the social media tally at the bottom of the video.

She felt like an idiot, putting herself out there again, only to be rejected. She stretched out in bed, laid back down on her right side, and hugged her pillow into her chest. How many times would she be taken in by Simon's easy smile and infectious laugh? She kicked her legs with irritation, knowing that she'd surrender if he took her in his arms again, and she'd be with him in only a few short hours. He'd said that he needed to stop by the speedway to visit his brother, Andy, in the morning on their way out of town. Hannah closed her eyes and tried to force herself back to sleep, wondering why they'd need to meet Andy at a speedway. What exactly was a speedway?

CHAPTER ELEVEN

"Would you like to stop for breakfast?" asked Simon, reaching for Hannah's bag in their hotel's casino lobby.

"No, thanks. I'm still stuffed from last night's buffet," she said, rubbing her belly.

He laughed, causing warmth to flow through her chest and sparking a desire to snuggle into his side, or at least hold his hand. She allowed her fingers to rub against his as he grabbed the handle of her bag.

"Thanks," he said with a nod as they walked outside into the bright morning sun, causing Hannah to squint. The dozen valets in black vests and red bow ties ran between parked cars, greeting incoming and outgoing guests.

"What are you thanking me for?" she asked.

"For letting me take your bag for you," he said as if it were obvious.

She wrinkled her nose. "Shouldn't I be thanking *you* for that?"

Simon handed a tip to the valet as the man ran around the car to open the passenger door for Hannah. "Only if you need the help, and you don't. You're allowing me to ..." He paused. "Take care of you. And I like that."

"Your car's already here?" she asked.

"I gave my number to the valet before I met you in the lobby. I didn't want to keep you waiting, especially if you were hungry."

As she stepped to get into Simon's car, she ran her hand down his bare arm to feel his skin against hers. "That's sweet of you." She'd told herself she wouldn't flirt with him, but she couldn't seem to stop herself. It was almost like her unchecked mouth had transferred to unchecked hands that couldn't resist touching him.

In less than twenty minutes, they pulled off the freeway into an area of Las Vegas that was still vacant desert—void of vegetation, commerce, industry, or residential property. The only thing within a one-mile radius was a large outdoor stadium.

"What do they do in there?" she asked. "Do they use it for rodeos?"

He threw his head back and laughed.

"I'm serious," she said, annoyed at his reaction.

He rubbed his chin and shot her an inquisitive glance as they pulled into the parking lot. "It's the Las Vegas Speedway. Andy's a NASCAR driver. I ... thought you knew that."

Her stomach turned, causing acid to rise in her throat. She swallowed hard. "Your brother races those fast cars? Don't people *die* doing that?"

"In the early days of racing, there were a lot of deaths, but there hasn't been a NASCAR fatality in almost two decades. They've changed some rules, but I believe the current safety record is attributed mainly to increased safety measures. Andy will explain it all to you before you head out. We're more likely to die driving on the road home than my brother is driving his car at 200 miles per hour on the speedway, inches away from thirty other cars on the track."

His words didn't calm her, especially considering they had a ten-hour drive ahead of them. She wiped the sweat from her palms onto her jeans and cleared her throat to relieve her dry mouth as they walked through the swirling hot air in the parking lot. It shouldn't make her nervous to simply walk into a raceway stadium. She took in a deep breath and reminded herself that they'd be meeting with Andy for only a few short minutes, then be back on the road. *On the road!* her mind screamed. She really wished Simon hadn't mentioned them possibly dying in a car accident on the drive home.

"Andy!" Simon shouted as his little brother swung open the gate to welcome them into the stadium. He wore a full-body racing suit, similar to what downhill snow skiers wore in the 1970s, but it was eighty plus degrees outside.

"It's nice to meet you, Andy. I'm Hannah," she said, extending out her hand.

He ignored her outstretched hand and pulled her into a hug. "Hannah, I've been waiting my whole life to hug you. And no one is going to sock me for it today." He raised his eyebrows at Simon. "Or are they?"

Simon pushed Andy back. "Not today," he laughed out.

"Why would someone sock you for hugging me?" Hannah said with a wrinkled brow.

Excitement sparkled in Andy's signature light-blue Grant eyes—the eyes that Simon hadn't inherited. "I'm just joshing. You ready for a ride, Hannah?"

"Ride?" she asked, even more confused.

"Didn't Simon tell you? He arranged for you to accompany me on an eight-minute ride around the speedway."

Hannah's heart stopped. She opened her mouth but couldn't speak.

Andy touched her arm and looked at her with concern. "You *want* to go on a ride, right, Hannah?"

"Of course she does," interjected Simon, grabbing her by the hand and pulling her behind Andy as he led them down a dimly lit cement hallway. "She's just in shock at the prospect of real speed. Right, Hannah? Let's get her suited up."

"I … I don't know about this," she stuttered out, her respirations increasing with every step closer to her untimely death.

They reached a counter with a woman who sized her up within seconds, then pulled a white jumpsuit from off a hanger and handed it to them. "Put this over your clothes. Just to warn you, it gets hot in there."

"In where?" Hannah asked, dazed, confused, and sweating profusely. What exactly had she signed up for? Simon helped her step into the suit, and before she really understood what was happening, she was stepping out onto the racetrack as someone placed a head sock, then a helmet onto her head. She held up a finger. "Simon, what am I about to do, and why?"

"You're about to experience Gs that not even NASA astronauts get to experience as they're being propelled through space. You want to do this. Believe me. Here's to one more check on your list," he said with a closed fist.

"What list?" she asked, as they pushed her into the passenger seat.

Andy looked over at her from the driver's seat with a mischievous smile, his eyes lighting up with joy. At least this was something he enjoyed. Maybe it wouldn't be so bad after all. She felt someone reach across her and buckle her into her seat, then shut her door.

"Is it always this hot in these suits?" she asked, pulling at the collar.

"No. it's usually much hotter. Imagine these suits in July. Now hold on," he said with that same mischievous grin seconds before her eyeballs suctioned to the back of her head, vibrating in her skull like a pinball in an arcade machine.

Her entire body shook; she wasn't sure if her shaking was from fear or speed. She opened her mouth to scream, but all that came out was a high-pitched vibrato, something similar to what she'd heard an opera singer belt out once, but Hannah wasn't singing and it came out more like a terrified whimper.

"You okay?" Andy's calm voice resonated in her helmet.

His voice soothed her. "I am when you talk to me. How can you see anything? The view from my perspective resembles a Monet painting."

He laughed. "You ready to go faster?"

She closed her eyes and clutched her hands into fists as her adrenaline spiked even higher. "What?"

"Just kidding. Isn't this thrilling?" he asked as they rounded a turn.

"If I'm still alive when it's over, ask me that again. I don't think I've ever been so terrified in my entire life."

"You've got personality, Hannah," he laughed out. "I sure love your sense of humor. Now for the real question. Are you going to marry Levi, or Simon?"

With the mention of Simon's name, his laugh entered her mind and quieted her nerves. She focused straight ahead on the curved road and slowly breathed in through her nose, filling her chest to capacity before exhaling. A smile curved up her lips at the corners. "After this thrilling ride you've given me, Andy, I thought I'd marry you."

"Wahoo!" screamed Andy. "Did you hear that, Simon? I get Hannah!"

"No, Andrew. You don't," echoed Simon's irritated voice through her helmet, loud and clear.

～

*A*ndy wasn't allowed to crush on Hannah, but Simon couldn't blame him. And since Levi wasn't around, it was likely all the brothers would at least flirt with Hannah a little if they got the chance. Simon tapped his foot on the cement floor under the bleacher overhang as he waited for Andy to slow from their last run.

The moment the car came to a full stop, Hannah climbed out of Andy's car and stumbled toward Simon with purpose. He had to blink to be sure his eyes were seeing what he thought they were. Did that mean she'd chosen him? He jogged to meet her.

She barreled into his arms. "I did it! I came and conquered!" she yelled out in a shaky voice.

His chest swelled with pride. "Yes. You did, Hannah," he said with a laugh, then pressed his lips to her forehead. "Congratulations. You're now an honorary NASCAR racer, and I have it all on film."

"What about when I asked Andy to marry me? Is that on tape as well?"

Simon raised his brows. "That's complicated, since you've already asked me to marry you."

"What do you mean, I asked you?" she said with a faint smile before her face blanched and her body went limp.

Simon grabbed her under her arms, preventing her from falling to the cement floor. He screamed to Andy, "Call 911!"

Speedway first responders were at their side within

seconds. They laid her down on the ground and did a series of tests.

The first responder said, "Her vitals are good, but we'll want to have her checked out at the hospital. Let's get this suit off her."

"What do you think happened?" asked Simon, kneeling down next to Hannah.

Andy reached down and touched Hannah's forehead. "It's not the first time a beautiful woman has fainted after being in a car with me."

"Oh, get over yourself," said Simon.

"I think she's dehydrated," Andy said to the ambulance medics who jogged in with their stretcher. "Can you get her on an IV?"

"Why do you think she's dehydrated?" asked Simon.

"It happens," said Andy, whipping out his phone and texting someone.

"This is serious," said Simon, pointing at Hannah as they placed her onto the stretcher and started her IV. "Why are you on your phone?"

"I'm transferring some money to the boys—although maybe I should transfer it to myself, since she said she wants to marry me." Andy patted one of the medics' shoulders. "She'll be fine, right, guys?"

They all nodded, saying something about her needing rest as she smiled up at them weakly and was wheeled away.

Simon followed a few steps behind the stretcher. "You bet the guys today?" he asked Levi with irritation. He wasn't sure if he was more upset about his brothers betting on what would happen with Hannah, or about the rest of his brothers putting their money on Levi and not him.

Andy scratched the side of his face. "Let's face it: ending up in the emergency room at the end of a date would qualify as a loss."

Simon didn't appreciate Andy suggesting he'd failed.

"I need to pay up now," said Andy, raising his phone in the air as they followed the stretcher to the ambulance, "because the bet is double or nothing going into your hockey date tonight. My money's still riding on you, so please don't screw it up."

"How can you go wrong with a little ice skating and hockey?" asked Simon, leaving Andy behind and sprinting to catch up as they loaded Hannah into the ambulance.

They arrived at the hospital fifteen minutes later. The moment they entered the ER, two hospital staff members wheeled Hannah back to a room and transferred her from the ambulance stretcher to a hospital bed.

"Remind me to take an ambulance to the hospital the next time I need to go," Simon said with awe. "Talk about efficiency."

Hannah reached her hand out to him and stared up at him with pleading. "Don't leave me." Her face had regained its color, but she still seemed groggy.

"Never," he said with a smile, loving how she wanted him by her side. "But I heard them saying they'd be taking you back for a CT scan in the next hour."

"Right now, actually," said someone in scrubs who walked in the room with a clipboard in hand.

"I'll be here waiting for you," said Simon.

As they pushed Hannah's bed out of the room, she thanked him with a slow blink and a nod.

Simon sat in the tiny, cold emergency hospital room, waiting for Hannah to return from her CT scan, when he received a text from Levi. The text contained a three-second video of Hannah slapping Simon's face at the Carla Dean concert, then a clip of Hannah being wheeled out of the speedway on a stretcher. *How's Hannah? Need some help taking care of her?*

Simon didn't respond to Levi's text. He was too upset. If he'd known how the tests were going on Hannah, then maybe Levi's text wouldn't have bothered him so much. Simon had dropped the ball, and it weighed down on him in the form of guilt. He should have been watching out for Hannah, making sure she stayed hydrated.

A middle-aged female physician entered the room. "Good news: no concussion, but we're going to give her another IV bag of fluids before she's discharged. I'll have the nurse start preparing those discharge orders now."

Simon sighed out his relief. "Thank you, doctor. So, Hannah's okay to play hockey tonight?"

The doctor removed her reading glasses and looked at him in earnest. "She plays hockey? I wouldn't have guessed that."

"Don't tell Hannah that. She's tougher than she looks, and she's an adrenaline junkie."

The doctor returned her eyeglasses to her face. "Yes, she can play hockey," she said with a confused shake of her head. "She has no restrictions."

Simon thanked her again as she left the room.

A few minutes later, Hannah sported a wide grin as they wheeled into the room. "I'm glad that's over," she sighed out. "Can we go? Wait …" She looked down at her hands. "I'm not sure I'm ready to get back into a car right now."

Simon ran his hand down her arm to comfort her. "It'll only be a short drive. I'm ordering us a ride to the airport."

Her face relaxed as she settled back into her bed and the nurse attached another bag to her IV. "But what about your car?"

"You let me worry about that," he said with a soft smile.

Hannah's brows knitted together. "And what if there are no available flights into Sun Valley?"

"Then we'll take a helicopter," he stated matter-of-factly.

Her eyes grew wide with excitement. "Really? I've always wanted to ride in a helicopter. I thought about that the other day when I was at lunch with Annie."

"But the Terrences have a jet, not a ..." He snapped his fingers. "That's right, they do have a helicopter they keep in Costa Rica. And it's brand-new. I was never in their last one —something about it having problems at takeoff, and that's how they discovered Ariana's brain hemorrhage."

Hannah's mouth dropped open. "Ariana had a brain hemorrhage?"

"And she swims with dolphins. They invited us down next week. Do you want to go?"

She sat up and ran her fingers through her hair, causing Simon to wonder how she could be so beautiful sitting in a hospital in one of their frumpy plaid gowns. "Down to Costa Rica? Just like that? What about work?"

"Laptops and internet. You can't pass up an opportunity to ride in a helicopter and swim with dolphins."

"Is this really what life has always been like for you? To be able to go anywhere, anytime, without any worries about how you'll pay for it or if you'll lose your job or fail a test?"

"Pretty much." He nodded. "But my mom would say, 'With privilege comes responsibility.' I'm still learning how to be a good steward. I'm hoping you can help me with that, Hannah."

She scrunched her nose. "And how are you hoping I'll help you, exactly?"

"Let's not worry about that right now," he said, touching her hand. All he wanted to do was lean over and kiss her, but the reminder text he'd received from his mom last night after the concert ran through his mind. He'd promised to show some restraint and take things slow with Hannah, at least slower than he wanted. Levi had been in love with Hannah his entire life. Although Simon's feeling for Hannah couldn't be quenched, he'd only been in love with her for a month. He owed it to his brother to at least try and temper his passion. He twisted a lock of her hair. "Let's get you home so you can relax first. There are some performers in town with the ice show who'll be practicing on the rink tonight. It'll be fun to go watch them." He left out that his brother, Jimmy, had agreed to teach Hannah how to be a professional hockey goalie—he'd save that little surprise for later.

"That sounds wonderful. I'm ready to fly home to our little refuge where life is quiet, calm, and beautiful."

"Me too," he said, eager to knock two things off Hannah's bucket list in one day. *And Levi thinks he knows how to take care of Hannah. He's about to get royally schooled.*

CHAPTER TWELVE

*H*annah clicked on the incandescent light in her closet—one of the last of its kind. She loved its soft, romantic glow. She hadn't been this far back in her walk-in closet in ages. The long, thin area was stacked with folded clothes and large wicker baskets that held miscellaneous papers, belts, and sundries. The back of her closet was where she'd always stuck stuff she no longer needed or used but held sentimental value—things she wanted to show her kids someday.

She stood on the old wooden chair that adorned her closet and reached up to pull down a large carton from off the top shelf. Dust sifted down like snowflakes as she wiggled the box free. She managed to pull the container down without it hitting her head. It almost felt like Christmas morning as she slowly carried the box to her bed, set it down gently, and lifted its lid to find her white ice skates and the red Swarovski studded dress she'd worn at her last competition in tenth grade—the last competition her mom could afford to send her to. She'd packed the box almost ten years ago, along with her dreams of becoming a professional figure skater. Figure skating was expensive, even for people who were affluent.

Simon had told her that they'd get out onto the ice tonight, but it didn't sound like he remembered that she'd been a competitive figure skater who'd taken Sun Valley to nationals. Still, that was in another life. Maybe her own kids would want to skate someday. If they did, money wouldn't stop them from accomplishing their dreams—she'd be the one working to make sure of that. She'd never allow herself to be in the position her mother had been in when Hannah's dad had left them.

Hannah had scraped, toiled, and sweated for everything she had. She'd sacrificed time with friends, sleep, and even relationships to get through college and law school. It just didn't seem fair that the Grants had had everything handed to them, but she couldn't fault them. A flash of guilt pulsed through her with the realization that she'd do the same, starting with figure skating. She understood the Grants on a new level: they were good people, doing amazing things with their money, and Simon had a passion for helping others. She admired the passion he put into everything he did. *If only he had that same passion for me—not sure how I would handle that one.*

Thoughts of rugged, reckless, passionate Simon taking her in his arms caused her body temperature to rise. She wiped the perspiration from her forehead; she didn't have moisture to spare today. That was the last time she'd fast so she could pig out at a buffet. Waking up disoriented on a stretcher had been one of her more embarrassing moments. Fainting in Simon's arms had been a culmination of dehydration, emotional exhaustion from her terrifying and exhilarating NASCAR ride-along, and simply being pressed against his firm chest. Luckily, Simon had no idea the effect he had on her, and she planned on keeping it that way. He was proving to be dangerous to her health.

She grabbed her skates, walked to her bedroom window, and stared outside at the view of her mountain. She held an ice skate to her foot. "Still a perfect fit," she said. "At least my feet haven't grown." She followed Mr. Grant's example and recited her blessings aloud as she stared out at the beauty in front of her. She loved the woman she'd become, and being poor was the reason she'd grown the way she had—the challenges she'd faced had brought out her inner grit. A light flickered in her mind: she'd been privileged to be poor. And poor was relative. Compared to the rest of the world, she was rich. Working with the Grant Foundation that short week had taught her that she was the lucky one. With a hop in her step, she grabbed her purse and ran out the door for the ice rink.

Fifteen minutes later, Hannah stepped up to the outdoor reception desk of the Olympic-sized ice rink. It opened up to a snow-covered lawn that would be filled with spectators on lawn chairs in a few weeks to enjoy a summer ice show. Three very competent skaters spun around on the ice, but that was unusual for a Saturday night; the rink was normally packed. She wrote the low numbers off to slack season.

"The rink's been reserved," said the ticket agent when Hannah slid her credit card to him.

She held up her skates and sighed. "These babies will be depressed to hear that."

He laughed an adorable teenage chuckle—where his voice still fluctuated between the low and high pitch. "Oh, you're with them," he said, motioning to the skaters on the ice. "Go ahead. Mr. Grant said to have you come on in if any of you showed up, but to let you know that he'll be needing half the rink tonight."

Simon was proving to be a *go big or go home* kind of guy.

"Thanks," she said with a smile, and she walked through the gate. It was easier not to explain to him that she was with Simon, not the professional skaters practicing for their upcoming show.

She sat on one of the many white benches surrounding the ice rink and laced up her skates. She'd come to the ice rink thirty minutes early to see if figure skating was like riding a bike. She wanted to take a few turns around the ice and refamiliarize herself with the rink before she made a fool of herself in front of Simon; the Grants were known as exceptional hockey players.

Holding a fist to her chest with nostalgia, she hopped out onto the ice. She smiled as she pressed her skates into the ice to gain momentum. As her speed increased and the cool wind hit her face, she remembered why she'd loved figure skating: it invoked a sentiment of freedom, strength, and beauty.

Turning to skate backwards, she decided to start with one of the easiest spins, the single salchow. She sprung into the air and did one rotation, landing it perfectly but on shaky legs. Her confidence would need to be reestablished before she'd try the more difficult ones, like the loop jump.

For the next twenty minutes, Hannah ran through her more familiar jumps and spins. She left the ice, slightly dizzy from her spins, and took a water break. Water was her new best friend.

"Hey there, stranger!" Simon's deep voice pulsed to her core, sending happy flutters through her body.

She turned and grinned at him, noting that wore the entire hockey getup. "Glad you could make it, slowpoke. I've been here for ages waiting for you."

"You've been *waiting* for me?" he asked with a seductive smile. "We'll see who's poky," he said, tickling her side with one finger and causing her to giggle.

"I don't think you're using that word right," she teased back. She knew she was flirting with him and told herself to stop, but she had a bad habit of not listening to herself when it pertained to Simon.

"Which word?" He raised one eyebrow. "Waiting, or me?"

She returned his raised brow. "Waiting, because I have a feeling I'll be *waiting* for you on the ice." She jumped up and sped across the ice rink toward the far corner.

"Oh, it's on!" he yelled.

The rough clacking of hockey skates against the ice grew louder behind her. Just before he reached her, she lifted into a spin and changed directions, causing him to skid to a stop. She sped around the ice rink once, then returned to find him frozen in place with his jaw slack. She skated around him three times, then said, "What? Did you run out of steam?"

"Believe me, steam is not the problem here," he said, pointing to his chest and smiling wickedly. "But I think a little lesson on how to be a hockey goalie is in order."

Before Simon had finished speaking, several men entered the ice, bumping into each other as they pushed their own pucks around. One man carried an extra helmet and goalie outfit in his arms. Hannah pressed a palm to her chest to alleviate her constricting heart. Her face tingled as every ounce of blood drained from her face ... then her arms ... then her legs.

~

*S*imon could've sat and watched Hannah twirl on the ice all day, but this night was about her and her bucket list, not about what he wanted. So far, Annie's plan had worked like a charm. The Carla Dean concert and NASCAR ride must've done the trick, because tonight Hannah was the most playful, relaxed, and flirtatious she'd ever been with him. He couldn't wait to see how much happier she'd be after her hockey lesson.

"Hannah," he said, motioning to the guy in the full goalie suit. "This is my brother James, but we call him Jimmy. He's a pro hockey goalie."

Jimmy removed his helmet and held out his hand to her. "Pleasure to meet you, Hannah."

She was slow and apprehensive in accepting his handshake, which didn't seem normal.

Simon grabbed her arm after she'd finished greeting Jimmy and pulled her toward the edge of the ice. "I'm not liking your coloring, Hannah." He turned and spoke to Jimmy. "I'm gonna get her some water. I don't want her to end up at the hospital again today."

"And you brought her to play hockey?" Jimmy released a friendly snort. "Someone always ends up in the ER when you jokers hit the ice."

Hannah's eyes grew wide, but she didn't speak.

"He's kidding," said Simon as they reached her bench. He rifled through her things until he found her metal water bottle. "Here." He twisted it open and handed it to her. "Will you please drink this?"

She stared straight ahead as she gulped down her water. When she finished, she wiped her mouth and looked up at him. "I don't think this is a good idea."

"But you'll have a blast. Is it because of my unsightly brothers?" He held his palms up. "I get how you'd love to be alone with me. I get that, but they're good guys."

She smiled and released a soft giggle. It looked like all she needed was a little encouragement. He would show her how fun hockey could be, and that his brothers were gentle giants. He'd sensed her hesitation with Jimmy, but he couldn't understand why; everyone took to Jimmy. Maybe her hesitation originated from Jimmy and Simon looking like twins; they had the same brown eyes, which starkly contrasted with their five brothers' almost translucent light-blue eyes. They all had a similar build, tall and sturdy, but their eyes made Simon and Jimmy stand apart from the rest.

If she were attracted to Simon, then she'd be attracted to Jimmy, and that needed to be dealt with swiftly. "Jimmy can be a little intimidating, but he's as soft as a snail."

"Snails are slimy, not soft," she said with a wrinkled nose, showing her disgust.

"I get it. He's slimy. Don't touch him and you won't get slimed."

Hannah looked up at him with an exaggerated roll of her eyes. "I think I can handle myself."

"Great," Simon said, clapping his hands. "Let's do this." He grabbed her hands and pulled her up from her bench and onto the ice. "If you start to feel faint, give me the signal."

She furrowed her brow. "And what's the symbol for fainting?"

"Hmm, in comic books it's a little corkscrew circle above the head."

Hannah laughed. "Are you sure you made it through law school?"

"Just Harvard Law." He shrugged. "They accept anyone."

"Anyone with enough money," she said with a competitive smirk.

He pointed at her. "There's the fire I love."

She blinked a few times and wiped her forehead with the back of her hand, her cheeks flushing to a beautiful shade of pink. "What?" she asked in a breathy voice.

He pulled her in, spinning them around in slow circles. She looked up at him with longing in her eyes. He bit back the insane impulse to kiss her. "There are so many things I love about you, Hannah, but the timing's not right."

She spun out of his arms with a huff and skated to Jimmy.

"I'm ready for my lesson," she said, looping her arm through his.

Jimmy looked at Simon with a smirk and skated with Hannah across the rink. If Hannah was trying to make Simon jealous, that was a good sign … a very good sign. Unfortunately, it worked. He had to find a way to get her away from Jimmy and into his arms again tonight.

"Hannah, we need to get your protective gear on!" Simon shouted across the rink, motioning to a bench, loaded with padding.

She glared askance, then nodded and skated to meet him at the bench.

"Look," he said, staring down at his hands as he grabbed the chest protector vest and lifted it up and over her head. "I think you misunderstood me."

She glanced up at him for only a moment before she adjusted her vest. "Are you leaving again soon? For another few years? Jimmy seems to think you will be."

Simon released a sigh. Jimmy was either making his move, or he was trying to win the bet he'd placed on Levi. Either way, Simon had to shift the balance on the table, a balance heavily weighted against him at the moment. "Yes, but not alone."

Her face softened. "And what does that mean, exactly?"

He touched her lips with his fingertips. "I think you know *exactly* what that means." Then he swallowed hard and avoided her gaze, staying his desire to kiss her.

"Stop messing with me," she said, smacking his hand away. She glared at him as she grabbed the rest of her gear and skated back out onto the ice.

It didn't look like Andy would be cashing out tonight, but Simon couldn't care less about any of their bets. His heart was being ripped out of his chest, and his brothers were watching it happen with congratulatory smiles on their faces. He pounded his fist into his palm. It was the perfect night for a hockey rumble.

CHAPTER THIRTEEN

"Square up with the shooter!" Jimmy shouted. "Gloves out!"

Hannah clenched her jaw and reluctantly opened out her chest to one of the Grant brothers as they skated into position and lobbed another puck at her. Lob wasn't the right word; barrage, bombard, blast, bomb, any one of those B words would be applicable. She wanted to use her own B word when addressing them, but she held her tongue. Aside from a serious bruise forming on her thigh, it looked like she might survive this disaster. It hadn't been as bad as she'd originally thought. The top of the goal was below her head, unless she was in the super low position.

How did I let Simon talk me into doing something so stupid ... again?

A puck whizzed through into the goal, grazing Hannah's shoulder and causing her to suck in a quick breath. She whispered a prayer of gratitude that she still had her front teeth. The pucks had come at her slow at first, but now they whipped past her at lightning speed.

"Stay still with your chest in line with the puck!"

instructed Jimmy from her side. "Bend your knees into the athletic position."

Stay still? Did the hockey goalie do anything during a game? She never remained still on the ice—that was a lot to ask of a figure skater.

"Drop to your knees into the butterfly position!" Jimmy shouted as a puck came in low to the ground.

She dipped her head and watched as the puck slid between her legs. The Grant twins gave each other high fives. She no longer feared the tiny pucks flying at her face; she wanted to stop the little suckers. She'd played it Jimmy's way. Now it was time to do this figure-skater style and wipe those smirks off the Grant brothers' faces.

"Hold on!" she screamed, holding out up her arms.

"You got your fill? Should we call it a night?" asked Jimmy.

"My fill?" she said incredulously. "No. I want to try something. I want your brothers to count to three, then try and get as many of those blasted pucks past me in the following ten seconds as they can. Deal?"

Jimmy scrunched his face up into a pained expression. "Simon said you were hard-core, but I can't let you do this, Hannah."

"I've never had so much padding on in my life, and you should see the jumps I used to do."

"These pucks will come at you fast, Hannah. And all at once."

She challenged him with a look. "Tell them no backing down or going soft on me. I expect them to do it."

He held up his palms in surrender. "Your call. I'll go tell 'em." Jimmy skated away and had a quick powwow with his brothers. They all nodded, except for Simon.

Simon's hesitation only fueled her anger even more. She was already ticked at him for leading her on and insisting that she do all these crazy things that freaked her out. He wasn't stopping this.

Simon skated up to her with a doleful expression. "Hannah, you're not—"

"Get out of the way, Simon, or this is gonna hurt. One!" she shouted, ignoring him and starting her crossovers into a lunge for the spin.

She held her arms out in front of her body and brought her gloves together. Where her hands normally pointed down at the ice, she held them up in front of her face and pulled herself into a quick sit spin, nearly sitting on the ice as she spun at a dizzying speed with her left leg extended forward. Her spin wasn't as fast as normal; the bulky pads slowed her down, but only slightly. A succession of clicks pelted her pads. Fortunately, the hits didn't hurt, not like that one mysterious puck that had snuck past a pad somehow and nailed her in the thigh earlier.

She slowly rose out of her sit spin, extending into a graceful exit. She glanced down at the goal. No pucks had made it in; they'd all been deflected off her as she'd hoped. "Yes!" she screamed, then turned around to face the brothers.

Their arms all flew into the air as they rushed her. Before she knew it, she was being carried in their massive arms, passed from one brother to the next as they hugged her in celebration.

One of the twins gave her an extra-long embrace. She still had a difficult time telling those two apart. They were the youngest and obviously looked the most alike. He said, "I thought Simon was insane when he asked us to come out and shoot some pucks at you, Hannah, but man, you're amazing. You got my vote. Personally, I think you fit best with Jimmy —and just think: you could move to Oregon with us."

Hannah's hands formed into fists. "Simon asked you to do

what?" She turned to search the ice for the miscreant but found Jimmy down on his knees in front of her instead.

"Hannah, you belong with me," Jimmy said, removing her gloves and kissing the tops of her hands.

She opened her mouth to speak, then froze.

Jimmy continued, "I've never seen anything like that, and you and me, we belong on this ice together."

"That's sweet, Jimmy, but ..."

Her eyes scanned the rink. Simon stood at the far edge of the ice rink with crossed arms and a scowl.

Jimmy's eyes followed her to Simon. Jimmy shook his head and sighed out his acceptance. "At least I'll be getting another kick-butt brother."

"Sister," she corrected him. "Never underestimate the power of a woman." She caught the gleam in his eye that said she'd just revealed herself, then she realized what she'd said and stumbled to fix it. "What I mean is you *want* a sister, because we're tougher, right?" she stuttered out.

"Right," he said, then hugged her. "But make sure you've got the right brother."

"Did I hear that she's choosing one of us? Because I want to put my name in," said one of the twins, pushing the other one out of the way as they skated toward her. "I'm Thomas, and it's spelled L-O-V-E."

"What he's trying to say is John, spelled C-H-O-O-S-E M-E."

Jimmy pushed them both back. "Idiots."

"I don't see *your* play working on her, Jimmy," said John, the slightly taller twin.

Hannah lifted her hand to stop them from bickering about who could woo her better. "Jimmy and I were just talking about how great it is to be a strong single woman, and I have no plans on changing that."

They all glanced over at Simon and laughed. Simon narrowed his eyes and puffed his chest out at them.

John draped his arm over Hannah's shoulders as they skated back to the bench. "I can't wait for you to come wrestle snakes with us in Florida, Hannah. When Simon told us you'd love it, I thought he was messing with us, but now that I see how hard-core you are, I'm stoked to get you into the Everglades."

Hannah untied her skates with wide eyes as John threw off his gear and squatted down. Her heart nearly pounded out of her chest when he explained to her, step by step, how to wrestle a python into submission. When he finished, she raised her hand above her head and did the little swirly thing in the air, the signal for passing out.

"No, Hannah, you don't want to hold your arm up like that," said John. "That's just inviting the snake to come and eat you."

Simon slipped next to Hannah on her bench and took her hand. "You okay?"

"I think I spun too much tonight. I need a long bath," she said, resting her face into Simon's shoulder and willing her stomach to stop churning from thoughts of being slowly eaten alive.

John looked between the two of them with raised brows. "And that's my cue to get lost," he said, jumping to his feet and bolting. "You win tonight, Simon."

Why did she have to mention a bath? Of course, with all the brothers vying for her attention tonight, John would say Simon had won over the rest of them. Maybe there was a therapist she could see who could help her learn how to check herself before she spoke.

"Can I take you home?" asked Simon, slowly stroking her hair back from her forehead as her face remained pressed into his upper arm.

"But my car's here."

"I know," he said in his deep, yet calming voice. "We can come back tomorrow and get it."

Her mind zipped through her schedule for the next day. Again, she spoke without checking herself. "Levi's taking me fishing tomorrow. I guess I can pick it up with him." She paused when Simon's body tensed. "I didn't mean to bring up—"

He tipped her chin back and stared into her eyes, clearing her thoughts. He slowly lowered his face until his lips brushed against hers. Tears of relief bubbled out the edges of her eyes as he whispered, "I'm sorry." She closed her eyes, allowing his breath to warm her. He slowly parted her lips, the moisture from his kiss elevating her heart rate. She bloomed in his arms, begging for him to continue to hold her, to kiss her, to touch her. Some people called it melting, but that's not how it felt to be in Simon's arms. His kisses caused her to bloom like a flower that hungered for sunlight, water, and another flower's pollen. What would happen when the sunlight, the water, and the pollen disappeared?

She pulled back. "What happens tomorrow, Simon?"

"Nothing. Let's keep kissing and not think about it." He reached for her, but she stood.

"I can't do the roller coaster with you, Simon. It's too bumpy. And scary. Really. Really scary. And Florida?"

He wrinkled his forehead. "Like scary *good*, right? And Florida was supposed to be a surprise. I thought you wanted this. I thought you wanted to travel."

"I love it here, Simon. This is home. This is stable. This is safe. You, Simon—" She pointed at him. "—are not."

Simon wilted into the bench, or she could have just imagined that. She grabbed her purse and ran for the parking lot, allowing her hot tears to flow unabashedly.

CHAPTER FOURTEEN

"*H*annah?" Her mother's voice echoed through her bedroom door. "It's a beautiful morning. Would you like to go to Sunday brunch with me?"

Hannah stretched out in bed, yawned, and turned to face the door. "I can't. I'm going fishing with …" She faltered. Maybe her mom didn't catch the *with*.

"Can I come in?" her mother asked in a soft voice. Her mom didn't normally speak to her in such a tender way, but when Hannah returned home last night bawling, her mother was there to witness the whole blubbering thing. Hannah hadn't gone into details, other than saying she'd been mistaken about someone and just needed some time to move on.

"Yeah," Hannah said reluctantly. She wasn't in the mood for a pep talk, but that's what she was about to get.

"You okay?" her mother asked.

"I'll be fine."

"When you fish, you're usually out before dawn." She tapped her thigh in thought. "And every other day. It's just so unusual for you to sleep in like this."

"It's the beginning of spring. The rivers are still too cold in the mornings; the trout won't be biting yet. But …" Hannah faked a smile. "If it's a good fishing day, I'll make you fish tacos tonight."

Her mom raised an eyebrow. "Have you ever known me to eat trout?"

Hannah released a grunt of laughter. "Have you ever known me to stop asking? One of these days I'll get you to eat fish."

"When I'm dead, you can bury me with all the trout you can catch. Until then, no fish."

"Well, that's …" Hannah squirmed. "Morbid."

"And unless you want that picture in your head every time you ask me, please stop asking me."

"You got it."

"So, who did you say you're going with?" her mother asked with an uninterested shrug.

Hannah cursed in her head. "I didn't say."

Her mother crossed her arms and stared her down. So much for being uninterested.

"Levi is picking me up in an hour."

Her mother's face lit up. "See, you've already moved on." She kissed the top of Hannah's head. "With your beauty, you'll always have options." She rubbed her palms together with excitement. "And Levi is probably the best option you'll ever have. You know you can marry more in a minute than earn in an entire lifetime?"

Hannah closed her eyes and rubbed her temples. "Please don't ever say that in public, and *never* mention Levi and me to anyone. We're just friends."

"Okay, sweetheart," she sighed out, sitting next to Hannah on her bed. "Just have fun today." She patted Hannah's leg and walked out.

Hannah sat up in bed, unsure what had just happened and

why her mother had dropped the subject. Whatever her reason, it made Hannah happy. The thought of spending the day outside on a beautiful spring day with her old friend helped her forget how she longed to be in Simon's arms. *Shoot!* He was in her thoughts again. She jumped out of bed. *I need to get moving and stay busy.*

An hour later, Hannah pulled her wet hair up into a ponytail and pulled her favorite Idaho Hawks baseball cap snug onto her head. The house was quiet after her mother had left to meet her friends for brunch. Hannah cringed, realizing her mom had exciting news about her little girl and the Grant boy to share. "Please don't, Mom," she said aloud as the doorbell rang.

Levi stood on her front porch with a grin. There was no misinterpreting Levi's facial expressions; there never was. "Morning, Hannah. Ready to show me the ropes?"

"Right," she said with sarcasm. "We used to fish together, remember? You can fish with the best of us women."

He raised an eyebrow at her as they loaded her tackle box and fishing pole into his trunk. "Does it always have to come down to a boy-against-girl thing?"

"Until you acquiesce? Yes."

Now both of his eyebrows rose. "And what would I be acquiescing?"

"That women are better in every possible way." She held up her chin as she jumped into the passenger seat.

"Whoa ho ho," he sang out. "Look who's so hoity-toity. I'll make you a bet. Whoever catches fewer fish today must clean them, cook them for dinner for the other person, *and* admits they are the lesser of the sexes."

"You're looking pretty confident over there," she said with a smile. "Why *is* that?"

He pointed to his chest. "This confidence has been earned. Let's just say that when people bet on me, they get a great return. Even when it seems like I'm losing, something grand happens. I've been sweating it these past few weeks, even last night, up until the very last minute—" He put a fist up in the air as he turned a corner. "—the miraculous happened and I'm back in the game."

Hannah gave him a quizzical look. "What are you betting on? Sports?"

His eyes grew wide.

"Are you a gambler, Levi?" she asked. "Betting is addictive, and you could lose a lot of money."

He waved a dismissive hand in the air. "It's metaphorical. I mean when other people bet on *me*. I'm not the one getting the money here. I'm just saying if you need to bet on something, *I'm* that something to bet on."

"You're not making any sense, Levi," she laughed out.

He sighed out something that appeared to be a mixture of relief and contentment. "I'm excited to start hanging out with you more, Hannah. We can check out our old stomping ground: the hot springs, the rope swing, the pizza joint in the old church." He patted his steering wheel. "It's gonna be great."

"You're right," she said, taking a deep breath and relaxing back into her seat with a wiggle. "There's no place like home. I can't wait to visit all the places I loved exploring as a kid. And together, it'll be even better."

He glanced over at her with the same boyish grin he'd sported on her porch.

"I plan on living here forever, spending every day hiking in these mountains, skiing, ice-skating, riding horses, getting together with friends," she said, patting his arm. "I can't think of a better place to settle down and raise a family."

"Hannah," he said, scratching his neck, "have you ever been to LA? This place is great, but why live here when you could live in LA, where it's sunny and warm year-round; in

San Francisco, where the city comes alive at night; or in New York, where you can experience cultures from every corner of the world? Hannah, think about the museums, the shows, the beaches, the endless entertainment, the amazing restaurants, the professional sports, the excellent medical care, getting dressed up and going to the trendiest places in town, having huge poolside parties with friends. It's barely warm enough in the summer here to even get into a pool."

"You sure like the city. I'm not saying I don't want to travel, but it's different living in a big city with all the violence, the filth, the smog, and mean people who think they can grab you—I get enough of them visiting here, thank you very much. If you love the city that much, Levi, you should live there. I'm not saying those places don't have wonderful qualities. I just don't see myself settling and raising my family in a big city, you know?"

Levi rubbed his cheek with his palm and stared out at the road ahead of him.

"It's not *that* thought-provoking," she said. "Now, if you want thought-provoking, tell me what possesses your brothers to hunt pythons in the Everglades. And how your mom is okay with that."

He turned to her with a shake of his head. "That's one story of many I could tell you about growing up in a household of crazy, energetic, and driven brothers."

"And I want to hear all of them," she said, hoping he'd omit the ones that included Simon. "Today is catch-up-with-my-old-friend day, and I want you to tell all."

"And you'll have to tell me about high school after you transferred schools and then college."

She glanced at him askance. "I worked with you for an entire year and you never talked to me, Levi. Why?"

Levi cleared his throat and shifted in his seat

uncomfortably, but he didn't look at her. "High school was a weird time."

"What was weird was having to wear those awful medieval French wench dresses at the Mandolin."

"That's how I remember you from high school. I thought you liked to dress nice and be social. Didn't you like those dresses?"

"You call that dressing nice? Maybe in a guy's fantasy." She wrinkled her forehead. "Are you kidding me? I'd never work at the Mandolin if that was still the uniform. I'm glad your family did away with those dresses. I spilled out of mine." She held an open hand out in front of her chest. "And I don't want to spill out of anything. I'm more of a baseball cap and waders kinda girl, like today." She motioned to her outfit. "This is me. I'd much rather be outside in nature, fishing with a good friend," she said, touching his arm, "than have to wear a cocktail dress and entertain in a stuffy room full of stuffy people. But you're right." She thought back to her teenage years. "High school was a weird time."

"Yeah." Levi took a minute to stare at her, then out his window. He tilted his head sideways and smiled. "Huh," he said, looking as if he'd just discovered the answer to world hunger.

"Having an aha moment over there?"

"I am," he said as an expression of awe crossed his face.

"I could use some of that understanding. Want to tell me why you ignored me that year?"

He scratched his jaw. "I was an idiot. But Pythons …"

She shivered but allowed him to continue with his brothers' adventures in the Everglades. They settled into easy conversation, which continued for the next two hours as they fished in the cold river water in their chest-high waders. She'd forgotten how fun, easygoing, and steady Levi could be, but as much as she thought she wanted and needed *steady*, she knew she wouldn't want to spend every day with Levi like this. It just wasn't as exciting as …

No, I promised myself I wouldn't go there. She needed to shift her focus to Levi as he wound his arm high above his head and executed a beautiful cast. The fishing line whirred as it danced in circles in the air, lending life to the serene landscape of Big Wood River. Massive cottonwood trees lined the river, standing like giants on the water's edge. Just beyond the river, snow-covered grasses would soon glow amber in the summer sun.

"You got skills, Levi," she said.

He nodded his thanks. "How many have you caught?"

She twisted her lips, not wanting to answer.

"Hannah?" he said with one raised brow.

"Three."

"Five." He did a little victory dance. "Which is the better sex, again?"

She laughed. "We're not finished yet. Don't be all smug. I haven't even given it my best bait."

"I'm good to stay out here as long as you are," he said with a smirk.

"On second thought …" she said. She could use the afternoon to run errands before her workweek started tomorrow. "I'm kinda hungry now. You good if we head back and I fry these up for lunch?"

"How about I take you to lunch? You can make the fish for us another night."

"Deal," she said, trudging through the water to the river's edge.

"I have another idea," he said, taking her hand to help her out of the water and onto the riverbank.

"What's that?"

"I'll still take you to lunch, then you can come over

tonight and fry the fish up at my house. We'll add trout to our family dinner."

"Family dinner?" Her body flushed. "Will your entire family be there?"

"My mom said something about it being the last dinner we'll all be together for before everyone heads out. She's pretty upset." He leaned against his car and looked at her with the sappiest puppy-dog face she'd ever seen. "You'd be doing me a favor by distracting her from the thought of having her boys leave home again."

"Guilt trip?" she said, removing her waders and throwing them in the plastic bin in his trunk. "That's what you're doing, guilt-tripping me?"

He shrugged shamelessly. "Did it work?"

"Yes." She sat in the passenger seat and crossed her arms. "Now feed me before I change my mind."

Four hours later, Hannah stood in Levi's bedroom with her mouth ajar. "This is a manor, not a bedroom. You could fit a rowing team in here, and their boat."

"It's the best bedroom in the house, right?" asked Levi, pressing his fists into his sides like a superhero.

She held back her giggles. "It's impressive," she said, but he hadn't shown her Simon's bedroom yet, and she wasn't about to ask to see it.

Levi motioned to his door. "Kitchen?"

"Yes," she said, relief washing over her. "We need to get cooking, or the trout won't be ready."

"Hannah Fields!" shouted Levi's mom as she walked into the bedroom. She epitomized class, from her confident posture to her relaxed, yet trendy blazer and jeans. Hannah hadn't noticed until then how much Simon resembled his mom. "I'm so glad you could come tonight." She put her arms around Hannah and squeezed. "It's about time someone my size came to visit."

Hannah smiled. "Thank you for having me, Mrs. Grant."

"Has Levi given you the grand tour?"

"Yes," said Hannah. "Your house is amazing."

Mrs. Grant gave a slight bow. "Thank you. Did he show you the aquarium? That was an engineering feat."

Hannah looked up at the ceiling in thought. "I don't remember an aquarium, but I've seen some really spectacular rooms."

"You'd know if you'd seen it," said Mrs. Grant. "Come on. I'll show you."

"Mom, we need to fry the fish," Levi interjected.

Mrs. Grant silenced him with a look, then took Hannah's hand like Hannah's mother had when she was young. "Dinner can wait."

Hannah had never felt so welcome in a home before. Mrs. Grant continued to hold her hand as they walked down the spacious hall that resembled an ancient Roman painting, with light mustard walls and rolling arches high above their heads. Mrs. Grant stopped at the large metal submarine door, complete with a red wheel handle that spun to open. Hannah stepped through the door into an underwater hotel.

Hannah spun in a circle, taking it all in. "This is amazing!" she said, pointing at the aquarium that occupied an entire wall. Then she turned and raised her hands to the large picture window with view of Bald Mountain on the second floor. "… and a mountain resort in one." She blinked her eyes a few times in awe. "Who came up with this idea?" she asked, stepping up to the fish tank and running her hand across the cool glass as a small shark glided by. She pressed her right hand into the glass as if a fish would come up and try to touch her from the other side.

"I did," came Simon's voice from behind her.

Her body tensed and her breath quickened; she couldn't move or speak. She stared ahead at the calming fish as they undulated through the water. She should've known this was Simon's room. Of course it was his bedroom. When she'd first seen the unique door, she'd wondered if Simon had picked it out. She cringed at how she'd been caught invading and admiring his most intimate space. She needed to find a way to slip out of his room without giving herself away like she had with Jimmy last night.

Simon's breath warmed the top of her head as he lightly pressed his chest into her back, causing her heart to race. Her eyes shot to the door in search of Levi and his mom.

"They left." Simon placed his hand over hers on the glass. "His name is Buttercup," he said as the shark swam by.

She swallowed and attempted to speak in a normal, unaffected voice. "You named your shark *Buttercup?*"

Simon brushed his hand over her left hip, then slid it across her stomach until he held her by her right side, hugging her gently into him from behind. His cheek touched hers, sending goose bumps up her arms. "I can't stay away from you, Hannah. I've tried."

She closed her eyes and happily bathed in the warmth where their bodies touched, but she knew the sunshine wouldn't last. Simon had done this to her time and again. She knew better than to think it would be different this time. "Seems you can't stay with me either."

"Is this what you want, Hannah," he said, squeezing her softly, "to be in my arms? Say yes and I'll tell everyone else know you're mine."

Her mind yelled *yes!* as his lips trailed down her neck. She tilted her head to the side, opening her neck to him. Her breath caught in her chest as he kissed her shoulder, sending chills down her spine. He continued with soft, moist kisses at the base of her neck and slowly made his way up to her ear.

"Hannah!" Levi called from the hall. "We started the trout."

She jumped away from Simon. She should be cooking with Levi, not falling into Simon's arms and under his spell again. "I need to go help Levi. I lost our bet."

"I think I'm the one that lost the bet," he mumbled as he picked up a piece of paper from off his desk.

"What did you say?" she asked, stepping into the hallway.

"You didn't answer my question," he said, following her down the hall. "Do you want to be with *me?*"

She formed her hands into fists, frustrated. She wanted to trust him, but how could she?

"Wait, Hannah," he said, waving the piece of paper in the air that he'd rolled.

"Planning on swatting a fly?" she asked, looking back at him with a raised eyebrow.

"Maybe," he huffed out, "if she doesn't stop running from me."

Hannah gasped as she spun around to face him. "You did *not* just call me a—"

"Hannah?" called Mrs. Grant from the kitchen. She must have heard them coming.

With an upturned nose, Hannah spun on her heels and marched into the kitchen, but not before Simon stuffed the rolled piece of paper down the back of her shirt and said in a hushed tone, "Don't worry. I didn't get a plane ticket for myself. This is about me finishing something I've started."

She turned around to ask him what he was talking about, but he'd disappeared. She pulled the paper from her shirt and unrolled it as she walked at a snail's pace into the kitchen. It was a printout of a plane ticket in her name to Costa Rica. Her mouth dropped open.

"Hannah?" said Levi from the stove as he placed a fillet of fish into the sizzling oil. "What's that? Are you okay?"

She furrowed her brows. "Why would Simon give me a plane ticket to Costa Rica?"

Levi shook his head. "Do you really need to ask why he'd invite you on a tropical vacation?"

Mrs. Grant looked between them with interest but didn't speak.

"But he said he didn't buy a plane ticket for himself." She shook her head. "I don't get it."

Levi and his mom exchanged a look that Hannah couldn't read; then Levi asked to see the printout. "Seat 3A," he said, rubbing his chin. "He's sending you first-class and scheduled a helicopter to pick you up at the airport when you land in Costa Rica to take you to Playa Flamingo, Meri Terrence's resort."

"Helicopter!" Hannah exclaimed, grabbing the paper out of his hands and scanning it again. She'd told Simon she'd wanted to go on a helicopter but hadn't told him that it was on her bucket list. This was a dream come true. She wanted to thank him, but how would she do that with how things were between them?

Levi put his arm around her shoulder. "I see you're excited and I don't mean to burst your bubble, but you lost our bet today and you're the one that's supposed to be cooking this fish, and I've already cleaned it and started frying. You gonna help me out here?"

Hannah laughed. "Sure," she said, picking up the spatula to flip the fish.

He bumped her side as she wiggled in next to him at the six-burner gas stove. "I'll talk to Simon tonight if you'd like and ask him why he's such a flippant weirdo."

"You do that," she said, leaning her head against his shoulder with a sigh. "You're amazing."

"Mom, did you get that on video?" he said, turning to look for his mom, but she'd disappeared like Simon had.

Hannah touched his arm. "Seriously. Thanks for always being so steady and reliable. I couldn't ask for a better friend."

"You're welcome. I'm so glad to hear that," Levi said, clearing his throat. "Because a friend who's steady and reliable is what I always hoped to be … to you. I mean, isn't that what every man wants?"

"Stop," she said with a smile, then reached up and kissed his cheek.

"Did you get that kiss, Mom?" he yelled out, causing Hannah to giggle. "Do you mind if I tell my brothers that it got sizzling in the kitchen tonight between the two of us?" he asked Hannah, pointing to the fish in the pan. "And that you kissed me and told me that I was *amazing*?" He spoke to her differently now than he had at the bowling alley.

She rolled her eyes at him and sighed. "Boys."

"You rang?" asked one of the twins as they strode into the kitchen together.

Hannah squinted in concentration to determine which twin was which.

"Smells good. Anything to snack on?" asked Thomas, the shorter one at 6'3" instead of his taller 6'4" twin.

She placed a hand on her hip. "Not to sound like your mother, but we're almost ready to sit down, and you don't want to spoil your appetite, because this trout is going to knock your socks off."

"No worry there," John laughed out, giving her a big bear hug. "We're always hungry."

She looked between the three brothers and grew nostalgic. She couldn't wait to sit down to dinner with the rest of the guys. Even with how confusing things had gotten between her and Simon, calm filled her breast. That's what this house was—the closest thing to the proverbial *home* she'd ever experienced. She glanced up at a decorative wooden breadboard above the sink that read, "If you seek the meaning of life, leave home. To find it, come home."

"I love that saying," said Hannah. "I want to hang that in my home someday."

"*Your* home?" Thomas scratched his neck. "I was thinking maybe Levi at first, then Jimmy because you two are amazing on the ice, then Simon, then back to Levi, but Andy just walked in the door and told Nate that he planned on marrying you—something about you asking him?" He clicked his tongue. "Nate said he didn't believe Andy and that you'd be much happier with an NFL star like him." Thomas patted his chest. "Remember, I've still got my name in there."

Hannah laughed. "Andy's here? I need to give him a hug."

John snapped his fingers. "So Andy, then? Why was all my money on Levi?" he said, pushing Levi.

Levi shoved John back. "Okay, boys, time to earn your keep. Finish the trout. Hannah's going to set this straight with Andy and Nate, and I need to get online for a minute before dinner." He walked out into the hall with Hannah. "Can I see that itinerary for a sec?"

She shot him a questioning look but allowed him to snap a quick photo of the page.

"Good to know your itinerary so I can get you to and from the airport." He pointed to himself. "Steady and reliable. Remember?"

She laughed and squeezed his hand before turning down the opposite hall.

"Let them down easy, Hannah. They're fragile men."

"Right, because you don't get much more fragile than an NFL star and a NASCAR racer," she said with heavy sarcasm.

"I'm glad we see eye to eye on this." His deep voice carried from down the hall, but she knew her voice wouldn't project the same, so she simply laughed to herself before her thoughts turned to the only man in the house she didn't see as a brother.

~

Simon stared down at his full plate as forks feverishly clattered against porcelain around him. Everyone was in good spirits tonight, even Hannah—which proved she didn't care about him. He was the only miserable one there. Annie had been mistaken; she'd told him that if he helped Hannah get through her bucket list, she'd fall for him. He raised his eyes just long enough to sneak a peek at her but caught Levi's questioning stare instead.

"How's the fish, Simon?" asked Levi from across the table.

Simon stabbed the charred fish with his fork and lifted it. "Seriously?"

His brothers erupted into laughter.

Levi shook his head. "Sorry. My mistake leaving the frying to the twins."

"You think?" Simon responded.

"This is my fault," said Hannah from the far end of the table, where she sat chatting with his mom. "I was supposed to cook the fish, and I dropped the ball. Here, Simon, eat mine," she said, holding up her plate to pass it down.

Before Andy could grab it from her hands and pass it along, Levi stood and said, "Here, Hannah, I'll trade you seats. You and Simon can share from across the table."

The room fell silent as everyone shifted their focus to Levi and Simon. Simon narrowed his eyes at Levi, wondering how his brother planned on sabotaging him. With Levi surrendering his seat, he was either removing his claim on Hannah, a claim he'd had since childhood, or he was planning something downright dirty—downright dirty was the most plausible.

Hannah seemed reluctant to take a seat across from Simon, which didn't surprise him in the least. It didn't matter that he'd said the timing wasn't right; he'd never said *they* weren't right together. It wasn't easy accepting that she'd rather spend the day fishing with Levi than spend it with him, and she'd run to Levi when he'd called. She chose to spend time with Levi in the kitchen over Simon in his bedroom.

"Thanks for the offer, Hannah, but I've lost my appetite," said Simon. "I need to prep a file for tomorrow anyway." He stood, turned, and walked to his bedroom.

A few minutes later, Simon sat on the edge of his bed with his eyes closed. He leaned forward and pinched the bridge of his nose.

"Simon," said Levi as he walked in through the doorway, "we need to talk."

"Not in the mood, Levi. Beat it."

"Bloody nose?" asked Levi stepping closer, which caused Simon's adrenaline to kick in.

"Yeah. Want one? It'll only take me a few seconds, and it would be very rewarding."

"How about I give you this instead?" Levi said, handing Simon a piece of paper.

Simon sat up and scanned the paper. "You bought me a flight to Costa Rica? Is this a joke, Levi?"

"No. She wants you, not me, and I think I'm finally okay with that. I'd been stuck in a boy's fantasy since high school."

Simon's mouth went dry. "She told you that she wants *me*?"

"Not in words," said Levi. "And I never said *want*. But there's not a doubt in my mind that she loves you."

Simon jumped up from his bed and threw a fist in the air before embracing Levi.

Levi laughed. "I think I'll take a break from the game."

"Not if Annie has anything to do with it," said Simon.

"I think you mean Mom. I'm starting to think she's orchestrated this from the beginning. And by the beginning,

I mean elementary school. I think she's always wanted Hannah for a daughter—more than we've wanted Hannah to be ours."

Simon shook his head. "Not possible."

Levi slapped Simon on his back. "Then go get her."

Simon ran for the door, then stopped short. "The timing has to be perfect."

"And by that, you mean you need to get Hannah into a position where she can't run and has no choice but to listen to you."

Simon rubbed his chin and pointed at Levi. "Exactly. Mom was right: you and I do think alike."

"Aren't moms always right?" said Levi with a broad smile.

CHAPTER FIFTEEN

*H*annah ran her hands across her cool leather arm rests as energetic passengers stepped down the plane's aisle. They must've been as excited as she was to be traveling to Costa Rica.

She glanced across the aisle at a handsome, toned man in a business suit, maybe ten years older than her. When she caught his eye, she smiled out of sheer excitement for her vacation. By his seductive grin, she quickly realized that he took her smile as an advance.

"Traveling alone?" he asked.

"No, she's with me," said Simon in the lowest voice she'd ever heard him use. He handed his bag to the flight attendant, then stepped over Hannah's legs to the window seat.

Her neck flushed. "You're tricky. So, you lied to me about not buying a ticket?"

"The real question is, do you want to kiss?"

She suppressed a laugh. She knew that if he leaned over and kissed her, she'd turn to putty, so she leaned away from him instead and narrowed her eyes. "It's been two weeks since you gave me this vacation, and you've barely spoken a word to me since then, and now you want to kiss?" She paused for effect, raising her eyebrows. "Take the new girl away for a weekend from inquiring eyes, make her feel indebted to you, then dump her like a sack of potatoes when you get back. Is that it?"

"I like the Idaho reference there, but no, I'm in this for the long haul. And how are you a new girl? We've known each other since we both had baby teeth."

"I meant I'm your new future conquest."

"I like the *future* part of that sentence," he said, popping a mint in his mouth and looking out the window as their plane backed out of the gate. "And yes, it's too late to leave the plane. They'd arrest you if you tried to get off now."

"So you're not denying that this is a setup?" She waved a hand in the air. "You think I'm going to fall into your arms and agree to a quick romantic weekend trip with you?"

"I'm not after a weekend with you, Hannah," he said in a hushed tone. Their eyes locked for what seemed like forever before Simon took her hand. "I'm simply after *you*. I don't expect you to trust me right now. I won't make any moves while we're there. This is about you having thrilling experiences. This is about you coming closer to understanding what the meaning of life is for *you*." He brushed her hair away from her eyes, causing her lips to tingle with desire. "I want you to be happy, Hannah, with or without me. Preferably with me. I'm not gonna lie; there is a selfish side to this. But I'll be a perfect gentleman ... if you want me to be." He rubbed his hands together and picked up the menu. "Now that you know what my intentions are, and that I won't pressure you, let's have some fun. And it all starts with food."

She relaxed, choosing to trust him this time. "It always comes down to food," she laughed out.

He held a finger in the air. "And water," he said to her, before turning to the flight attendant. "Can we get a few bottles of water, please?" He lifted an eyebrow at Hannah. "I'm not making that mistake again. You're drinking two bottles, right now."

"I'm going to be spending half the flight in the bathroom if you waterlog me," she argued.

He laughed. It was the first time she'd heard him laugh like that since their drive to Las Vegas. She wanted to press her ear to his chest and feel the jubilant rumblings. She'd forgotten how much she'd enjoyed listening to him laugh.

"Bottoms up," he teased, handing her a bottle of water.

She cupped the bottle, allowing their fingers to intertwine for a few seconds. Their eyes met and she smiled at him, letting him know he was on his way to winning her affection.

During the five-hour flight, she thought up every funny experience and story she could think of to make him laugh. He related several experiences as well, but they always had a part where he'd show emphasis by grabbing her hand, running his fingers down her arm, or playing with her hair. By the end of the flight, she held his hand while her legs draped over his lap and her head rested against his shoulder as she napped. She'd failed miserably at not falling into his arms, but at least she hadn't reached up and kissed him like she'd thought about doing a hundred times during the flight.

They deplaned and located the waiting helicopter within thirty minutes of landing. Thankfully, they passed two bathrooms on the way to the helicopter, which would prevent her from being uncomfortable during the helicopter flight.

Hannah shivered with anticipation as they stepped up into the helicopter.

Simon took her hand and helped her into the cockpit.

"You're shaking, Hannah. Are you sure you want to do this? I wouldn't want to force you to do anything that frightens you."

She would've laughed at the irony and called him out on it, but the rush of excitement overruled every other emotion. She sat to the left of the helicopter pilot and tried not to bounce in her seat with anticipation.

Once the pilot had repeated some commands from the air traffic controllers, the helicopter shot straight up like an elevator, but this elevator didn't stop; it just kept climbing into the air until it changed course and flew straight ahead. Hannah appreciated Simon giving her the front seat with a full view of the ocean, the rivers, and the cloud forests, but she would've liked to have held his hand during the breathtaking flight. On second thought, flying that high in the atmosphere and touching Simon, maybe even kissing him out of sheer excitement, might have tipped the scale and caused her to faint. She had no intention of visiting the hospital during this trip.

She looked back at Simon and mouthed the words, "Thank you."

"You're welcome," he said into the helmet, which she heard loud and clear, reminding her of her NASCAR ride-along.

They landed on a pad at the Meri's Flamingo resort, enjoying the first few minutes of sunset from the air. Simon grabbed her by the waist to help her out. She locked her hands around his neck, resting her arms on his shoulder, and smiled at him as he slowly lowered her to the ground, staring into her eyes with intensity. She could feel his heart pounding as she slid down against his body, ultimately resting her head against his chest like she'd wanted to do since their plane flight. He placed his hands on her back, not attempting to move away from her, but also not caressing her or trying to kiss her. She regretted not kissing him when he'd first boarded the plane, because now she would have to be the one initiating all the physical contact, and she hated the idea of begging him for physical attention.

"Want to see the resort?" he asked.

"Can we eat first? I'm starving."

"It's not an award-winning Las Vegas buffet, but I think we'll be able to find some decent food to fill you up."

Hannah laughed as she pulled her hair down from its ponytail and shook her head out, loving how the misty ocean breeze showered her face in its sticky droplets and ruffled her hair. She removed her shoes and stepped into the cool sand. "I haven't felt sand in my toes in years," she said.

Simon cupped her chin and looked at her with eager eyes, as if he was going to kiss her, but he pulled back at the last second, leaving her breathless and frustrated. "Let's leave our bags at the front desk and feed you."

"Yes, feed me or there's going to be trouble," she said, scanning the beach for food. She found an oceanside atrium with a restaurant inside. "There's our ticket." Out of the corner of her eye, she saw someone running toward them with open arms.

"Hannah!" Annie screamed as she embraced her. "I'm glad you made it."

"This is fun," said Hannah. "I didn't know you'd be here."

"Are you kidding? I wouldn't miss this adventure. We set out at five in the morning. Don't forget your suit," she said with a wink.

Hannah had forgotten about Annie's winks. She shot Simon a questioning look. "Simon?"

He ran pinched fingers across his lips. "Mum's the word. It's a surprise that you're going to love."

She'd been on a helicopter ride and was on a gorgeous beach in Costa Rica with the most attractive man on the planet. She couldn't imagine this weekend getting any better, but she couldn't wait to see what they had planned for her in the morning. She needed a picture window right now to shout out her blessings.

~

*S*imon stepped out onto his balcony at one o'clock in the morning. He leaned into the railing and stared at the crashing waves, praying that the sea life would cooperate in a few hours. Five a.m. couldn't come fast enough. He'd known he wouldn't get much sleep tonight, so he hadn't even tried. He hadn't had a restful night in almost two months, not since Hannah had walked in the door at the Mandolin.

He'd almost won her affection, but not yet. He hoped their ocean swim would tip the scale in his favor. After their swim with the wildlife, he'd take her in his arms again. He'd told her that he wouldn't make any moves on her during their trip, but she'd given him all the signs that she wanted him to, and he didn't have much willpower left. She either loved him, like Levi had said, or she didn't. He would know in a few long hours.

CHAPTER SIXTEEN

*H*annah woke to a door chime. She blinked her eyes open, wondering why she wasn't in her bedroom. Once she'd established her bearings, realizing she was in Costa Rica and had an excursion planned that morning with Simon, she jumped out of bed and rushed to open the door. "You weren't joking about five a.m.," she said with a half laugh, half yawn as she opened the door to Simon, who looked as smart and handsome as ever. "Can you give me just a minute to get dressed and brush my teeth?"

"Good morning," he said, leaving the door slightly ajar as he reached for her, pulling her into a hug and spinning her around. "I can't wait to get out onto the water with you, in our swimsuits."

She patted his shoulder and laughed. "And you're going to love my swimsuit."

He held her gaze. "Want to show me now?"

"No way. I have my surprises too." She tsked her tongue at him as she walked to the bathroom. "Why are you so awake at five a.m.? You're not usually in the office before eight."

"How do you know when I come into the office? Have you been stalking me?"

She laughed, loving how he could make her smile that early in the morning. "Can you tell me what we're doing this morning?"

"You'll see when we get there."

"Snorkeling?" she asked.

"I'm not giving it away."

"Fishing?" she prodded with excitement. "Now that would be amazing, to swim with deep sea fish."

"You couldn't get it out of me if you tortured me."

As she rinsed her mouth, she remembered Ari and Kai mentioning their boat. "Sailing?"

He was silent.

"Yes!" She jumped up and down. "We're going sailing."

"I never said that," he said, straight-faced.

"You didn't have to," she said with airs as she left the bathroom with her swimsuit under her clothes and her teeth brushed. "What do you think?" she said, blowing a minty breath in his face. "Better?"

His eyes bored into hers with desire. He wrapped his arms around her back and pulled her up and into him, causing her to gasp seconds before he kissed her with all the passion she'd known he possessed and hoped he'd channel to her someday. Her fingers grasped the hair on the back of his head, and she kissed him back.

"Where's my paper?" echoed a concerned voice through the room.

Hannah's eyes shot to the doorway, where Annie leaned against the doorframe.

Annie pulled a pen out of her messy bun and chewed on the tip as she gazed across the room at them. "You two may have just gotten me writing romance again." She sighed and turned in a circle, looking down at the stone floor as if she'd dropped her notepad. "I'm going to run down to the lobby and find some paper. Feel free to keep going, but you've given me enough inspiration to write an entire novel with that—" She patted her chest. "—one breathtaking kiss. Seriously, my eyes are misting over here." She stuck her pen back into her bun and fanned her face with her hands as she hurried toward the front desk.

Hannah buried her head into Simon's chest. "That was embarrassing."

"No. That was …" he said, tilting her head up by her chin and searching her eyes. "Perfect."

She released a sigh of contentment. "Can we do that again later?"

"Try and stop me," he said with a raised eyebrow. "But first, there's a sailboat with your name on it."

She followed him out of the room and down the hall. "Are you sure it's got my name on it? Because I'll be really disappointed if it says something cheesy on the side like Sirena."

He laughed. "I sure hope we don't encounter any mythical sea creatures when we dip our toes in the cool ocean water," he said with wide eyes, teasing her. "Wouldn't want to get dragged down to the bottom of the sea."

"Dip our toes in, like off the side of the boat?" she asked with a hurried breath, her anxiety mounting with each step closer to the deep ocean. They walked outside as the first rays of sunshine broke through the clouds, lighting the horizon like a child's watercolor painting, with long, fuzzy pink and blue brushstrokes.

He smiled. "You're going to love sailing," he said, pointing out to a boat at the end of the pier as they stepped onto the beach. "There's nothing quite like it."

"Sailing *in* a boat. Yeah, I can do that," she affirmed, telling herself that sailing off the Costa Rican coast in the arms of a gorgeous billionaire who loved her would be the ultimate fantasy for most women. But she'd only guessed Simon loved her by the way he kissed her. He'd never told her that he loved her. All he'd said was that he was in this for the long haul. For all she knew, he could be preparing himself to take off at a sprint the moment they touched down in Sun Valley.

Simon took her hand as they stepped up onto the pier. "I want to make this day special for you, Hannah."

"Thanks," she said with a sleepy smile. The little energy she'd had that morning had been zapped from entertaining her fears of sea predators and uncommitted men.

Kai and Ari welcomed them onto the boat. "Where's Annie?" asked Ari.

"I'm coming!" shouted Annie as she ran up the deck, waving a notepad in the air.

Ari sighed. "Let me guess. She caught you two kissing?"

Hannah and Simon looked at each other and laughed.

"She is enthusiastic; I'll give her that," said Kai, his sea-foam-green eyes glowing in the morning sunlight.

Annie took in a deep breath as she sat, stretching her arms out along the back of the white-and-blue bench. "Do you smell that earthy, almost foresty smell? I love this boat's scent and how it contrasts the effluvious tang of the sea."

Ariana scrunched up her nose. "I'll give you effluvious, but I don't think foresty is a word, Annie."

Hannah sniffed the air. The boat did give off a faint pine aroma.

"It is now," said Annie. "Did you know that Shakespeare coined several hundred words and phrases?"

"The scientist and the artist," Kai said in an aside to Hannah. "These girls can go at it for hours. Don't get them started about meat."

"I've had a *taste* of that conversation when we met for lunch," Hannah responded to Kai.

"Bravo, Hannah," said Annie. "Spar with us."

"How did you hear that?" asked Hannah. "I said that in my softest voice."

Annie shrugged. "Paxton has this almost supersonic hearing. I guess he's rubbed off on me."

"I don't think it works that way," said Simon with a laugh.

"I don't mean my hearing has improved. I simply pay closer attention now to what is being said, not only to what I see, as I'd done in the past. I've always been an observer; now I listen closely as I observe. I guess you could call me a behavioral *scientist*." She raised her eyebrow at Ariana as if challenging her to a game of wits.

Hannah found their dialogue intriguing, but she had no interest in joining them. She snuggled into Simon's side and listened to Annie and Ariana "spar" as they sailed farther and farther out to sea until the shoreline disappeared completely from view. She closed her eyes and held Simon's hand tight, listening to the seagulls crow above her head. She bristled when the salty water spritzed her arms and face as they glided their way through the rolling waves and fell into a soft slumber to the boat's gentle sway.

"We're here," said Ariana with excitement.

Hannah blinked her eyes open and glanced around. She didn't see anything but water. "Here?" she asked.

"You ready to blow another goal out of the water?" Annie asked Hannah.

"I don't think this matches the context of that phrase," countered Ariana.

Annie sighed. "Let me handle the context. You call in your dolphin friends."

"Dolphins!" exclaimed Hannah. "We're going to see dolphins?"

"Not only *see* dolphins, Hannah." Ariana's face lit up with joy as she stepped to the edge of the boat and dove in.

Hannah's hands trembled. "What is she doing?"

"Swimming with the dolphins," said Simon, squeezing her hand. "Surprise! Come on. Let's go see if they're out there."

"Has Annie jumped out into the middle of the ocean like this before?" Hannah asked Kai.

Kai smiled with amusement. "One of our dolphin friends saved Ari's life. The two formed this unbreakable bond. He used to come close to shore. During one of his visits, we paid to have him tagged by a marine biology group who studies dolphin migrations, with the understanding that we'd have access to his GPS coordinates so we could follow him as he migrates around with his pod of twelve dolphins."

"Twelve? And they're right here?" asked Hannah, standing to scan the water. As soon as Hannah finished her sentence, a dolphin leapt into the air, followed by three more. She gasped, then pressed her hand to her mouth in astonishment.

"Wanna jump in?" asked Simon, removing his shirt.

Hannah blinked, then swallowed back her drool. She tried not to stare at his bare chest and ribbed abs, though she allowed herself to look for a few seconds at least. She'd never seen him in a tight shirt that showed his physique, but she'd assumed he had muscles by the way his chest felt against her body when he held her tight. For a moment she hesitated, wondering if she was chasing after the billionaire playboy like her mom had, and if she'd get burned the same way.

"You worried about getting cold?" asked Simon, touching her arm. "You've got goose bumps."

"I get goose bumps when Kai touches me as well," Ari whispered to Hannah with a quick glance at Kai.

Too much information, thought Hannah. "No. I'm plenty warm, thanks," she answered Simon, wiping the fresh perspiration from her forehead.

She needed the ocean to cool her down, and she felt a thrill at the idea of jumping into the unknown. The knowledge that it was just dolphins they'd be swimming with transformed her fear into excitement. Ari had swum with these dolphins before, and one of them had saved her life. Hannah couldn't get much safer than that in the ocean.

"Do you want to jump off the boat together?" asked Simon.

"Maybe, if you can handle this heat," she said, pulling off her wrap and throwing it at him.

Simon leaned back and whistled, then lunged for her, but she avoided him by stepping to the side, then diving into the water. He jumped into the ocean behind her. She flipped and spun underwater in circles, teasingly avoiding his grasp as the dolphins next to them zipped around, playing their own water games.

Simon found her arm and pulled her up out of the water. "What were you doing?" he asked, holding her tight to his chest.

Being pressed against his muscles caused her brain to misfire. She forgot they were in the ocean and sucked in a salty mouthful of water that burned her throat and made her cough.

"You okay? I'm getting a life vest on you," he said in a voice that bordered on angry, waving to Kai. "We should've been wearing them already. And we're not taking these off until we're back on land," he said, grabbing the life jackets Kai threw down to them. Once Simon had tightened her life jacket in place, he sighed. "Okay, now let's go have some fun with these beauties, and I'm not taking my eyes off of you."

"Promise?" she said with a flirtatious smile.

"With how that swimsuit fits you, that's a promise."

"You can't even see my swimsuit with this life jacket on. Why don't we take them back off?" she said, hoping he'd hold her against his bare chest again.

He shook his head. "No way. I love the fire in you,

Hannah, but sometimes your adrenaline junkie behavior scares me."

She huffed out her disappointment but decided to enjoy the marine life. She concentrated on the dolphins as they grazed her legs and side with their smooth skin. The water bubbled and waved when a dolphin swam close to her, weaving in and out and jumping out of the water in succession, as if playing a game of tag with each other. She smiled at their playful nature and marveled at their strength and agile movements through the water. "This is spectacular! Thanks for arranging this, Simon."

He nodded. "You're welcome."

"Hey, guys!" yelled Ari. "We have a much bigger friend coming to join us," she said with excitement. "I've never swum with one of these giants before."

Hannah looked up, imagining a school of brightly colored fish or a few sea turtles were headed their way. She stared beyond Ari, but froze when she saw the massive, spotted form with a shark fin undulating through the water. Her body shook and she opened her mouth to scream, but she lost her voice. She squeezed Simon's hand and pointed at the large beast.

"It's just a whale shark!" yelled Ari. "They're vegetarian gentle giants who eat plankton."

With a nervous laugh, Hannah willed her head to stop spinning. "I think that was enough excitement for one day."

"You don't want to stay out here and swim with one of the biggest animals in the ocean? Wasn't that what you wrote on your card?" Simon asked.

Hannah's heart stopped beating. It was a good thing she was wearing a life jacket. She had a hard time pinpointing her exact emotions. She couldn't decide if she was angry that he'd tricked her into doing things that scared her, or grateful he'd helped her conquer those fears. "Now it all makes sense, but why were you having me do things that scared me? To conquer my fears? Shouldn't that have been my choice?"

"Fears?" he said with surprise. His eyes narrowed as he looked over at the sailboat. "I need to have a little chat with Annie."

"You didn't know?" asked Hannah, swimming beside Simon to the boat. "How could you not have known those were fears?"

"Who would be scared of a Carla Dean concert?" he asked as they reached the boat and he helped push her up.

"That was a joke," she said. "Who would want to wrestle a snake that was trying to eat them?"

"I have two brothers who do." With a shrug, he jumped up onto the deck.

"That's so wrong," she said with a shake of her head. "What about being hit with hockey pucks?"

"By the end of the night, you not only told my brothers to shoot them at you without holding back; you commanded them to, even after I'd tried to stop you. What was I supposed to think, Hannah? And the smile on your face as you stumbled out of Andy's race car solidified in my mind that these really were things on your bucket list."

She rested her face into her hands. "I can see how you'd think that."

Out of the corner of her eye, Hannah noticed Annie slap her hand over her mouth and start to descend the stairs to the cabin below.

"Annie, wait," said Simon in a stern voice. "I have a question for you."

Annie dropped her shoulders and said, "Sorry. I really thought that was your bucket list, Hannah."

"I'm sure we'll laugh about this someday," said Hannah with a tired shake of her head. She relaxed back into the cushioned bench and asked, "Did I seriously just swim with dolphins and a whale shark?"

Simon grabbed the back of her life vest. "I'm proud of you, Hannah. You came and you conquered."

Hannah sat up a little taller. "You're right, I did conquer some of my fears—but I still have two left to go."

"Two?" asked Simon. "I thought you only had to wrestle a large snake?"

"The other one has to do with you." She swallowed back her anxiety and rubbed her sweaty palms into her thighs, sticky with salt water.

Simon's eyes dropped to the floor of the boat as he took her hands in his and brought them to his heart. He bent forward, bringing his eyes level with hers. "Hannah, I've loved you since you walked into the Mandolin that night, thinking I was slow. And before that, I wanted to patch up your skinned knee and run with you through the forest."

"Wait," she said as the fuzzy memories became clear in her mind. "You comforted me when I fell down?"

He nodded. "Glad you finally remember me. Do you choose me, Hannah?"

"I always have chosen only you. This was never between you and Levi or you and anyone else. The thing is," she said in a shaky voice, "I run before I can get run out on. I avoid the conflict that will cause the most hurt. My worst fear, Simon, is not written on the fear card. My worst fear is that you'll leave me someday." She sat up tall. "But now that I've faced my other fears, I think I'm finally ready to face this one."

Simon's warm honey-colored eyes watered as he pressed Hannah's hands to his mouth. "I'm sorry I added to that fear, Hannah, and I know it's going to take some time trusting that I'm here to stay, but I love you and promise not to ever leave you."

She placed her hand to his cheek and searched his eyes for the truth. "I believe you. Can we pick up where we left off this morning in my hotel room?"

Simon ran his hand along the back of her neck and cupped her head as he slowly pressed his lips to hers. She tilted her head back and relaxed her body, allowing his soft, loving kisses to fill her with warmth that she'd take a chance on.

"Whoa!" said Kai, holding up a hand. "I know you two couldn't care less about the rest of us here, but this is not that kinda boat."

Ari raised an eyebrow at Kai.

"It's not that kinda boat right *now*," Kai corrected himself. "Why don't we get you back to shore and you can kiss all you want?"

Simon's face lifted into a full smile. "I heard somewhere that a couple should kiss to make up."

"Hold on," interjected Annie with an excited wave of her hand as she tapped her phone. She grinned when Carla Dean's song "Kiss to Make Up" blared through her phone's speaker. "I heard that the only way this will be truly effective is if you kiss through the entire song," she said with a wink. She handed her phone to Hannah while motioning for Kai and Ari to follow her below deck. "We'll be enjoying our lunch. We shouldn't need to come up for a while—unless the boat starts to tip," she said as they disappeared into the cabin.

"I have a feeling this won't be the last time we'll need to kiss to make up," said Hannah.

"I sure hope not, because I heard someone sing once how it's the best kind of kissing."

He pulled Hannah into his arms and held her tight. She gave herself to him willingly, trusting him with her heart as their lips spoke words of forgiveness, healing, and—most importantly—passion, Simon Grant style.

EPILOGUE

One Year Later

*H*annah swayed to Roy's sultry piano music as she grabbed a pitcher of water to refill her tables. She'd only worked at the Mandolin during the past year when they were short on servers, like tonight, and this evening's shift would be a snap because it was a simple buffet she was asked to merely oversee.

The Grants had opened the restaurant two hours early to accommodate the Terrence family, who'd rented out the restaurant to celebrate Kai's parents' wedding anniversary. The Grant boys slowly filtered in to enjoy the festivities, giving each other high fives and man hugs.

Simon bounced out of the kitchen with a huge smile on his face.

"What's got you smiling like that?" asked Hannah. "And my, don't you look handsome in your black suit and tie." She placed her hand on his cheek and rubbed the new growth on his face. She'd never thought she could be more attracted to him, not until that first time she'd seen him with a five-o'clock shadow that lent his face a more rugged look, matching his personality. He'd begun to grow out his beard again with a promise that he wouldn't allow it to become as unkempt as it had been when they'd first met, but she loved how it reminded her of their first meeting. "Wait," she said, glancing down at her watch. "We first met exactly one year ago today in this restaurant."

"It's been a year?" he asked, then reached down and gave her a soft kiss, causing her body to heat. "Happy anniversary."

She swooned as she blinked up at him, then realized all his friends surrounded them. "I have nothing to do. Why don't you let me bus tonight so you can catch up with your friends?"

He laughed, causing her to sigh. She never got enough of his laughter. "Are you kidding me? *Our* friends would rather catch up with you than with me."

"That's not true," Hannah argued.

"Yeah, it is, actually," said Kai, wrapping his arms around her in a big bear hug. "Annie and Ariana are looking for you. I think they're back there," he said, pointing to the far corner of the restaurant.

"Okay," she said, handing the pitcher to Simon. "I'll be back in a few minutes."

Hannah found Annie and Ariana dancing to Roy's upbeat blues as they took turns twirling Scout in circles. "This is exactly how I knew I'd find you. Festive as always." Then Hannah caught a glimpse of Ari's pregnant tummy. "Ariana!" she yelled. "Congratulations."

"Thanks," Ari said, leaning forward, out of breath. "I wanted to surprise you."

"It worked," said Hannah, giving her friend a hug. "I'm so

happy for you. And that would explain why Kai is so lively tonight."

"I don't know. I think Simon is about the most spirited man in the restaurant right now."

Hannah furrowed her brows. "Why would you say that?"

"Attention, family." Simon's voice bellowed through the speakers as the piano music cut. "I have a very special number to play for you for a very special lady."

Hannah pressed her hands into her chest as she spun around to find Simon seated at the piano. She knew he tinkered on the piano, but he'd never played for her.

"I've been keeping a secret from Hannah. I've been sneaking out and coming here to the restaurant to practice a song that I'd like to play for her tonight. Now, I'm not the best singer, but you all know this song, so please sing along when I give you the signal." He started playing a blues song that Hannah didn't recognize.

Annie pushed Hannah's back, prodding her to walk toward Simon. Hannah slowly stepped to Simon as tears welled in her eyes. Her arms began to shake, but luckily her mom was at her side, holding her hand as they stepped through the parted crowd.

Simon leaned into the microphone. "You've all been invited here tonight to celebrate a very special occasion. Hannah and I first met as children, but I first saw her as a *woman* ..." He paused until the applause died down. "I first saw her as a woman one year ago tonight. I know this may shock all of you, but it took some convincing to get Hannah to date me. On one occasion, when I was trying to impress Hannah, I told her that I had discovered the meaning of life from my extensive travels, but what I didn't tell her was that that epiphany didn't come to me until I looked into her green eyes and knew that *she* was the meaning of life, because she would bring meaning to my life. Hannah," he said, holding his hand out to her, "I'd like you to sit here with me when I play you a song."

Hannah's heat rose as she neared the piano. She took a seat next to him on the piano bench and smiled up at him.

"Before my song, I have something to ask you." He stood, then slowly kneeled in front of her, not allowing his eyes to leave her. Cries and gasps circulated the room as he held her hands in his. "Hannah Fields, you are the only woman I've ever loved and the only woman I ever want to love. I promise to cherish you and you alone for eternity if you will be my wife. Will you marry me, Hannah?"

The room fell silent.

"Yes," she said in almost a whisper, trying to catch her breath.

Simon jumped up, lifted her off the piano bench, and spun her in the air to the cheers of their family. "I owe you a love song. I think you know the song 'Kiss to Make Up.'"

"I think you owe me a kiss first," she said with a smile. "Simon Grant style."

"Now *that* I can do," he said, holding her so that her face was just above his.

She placed her hands on his cheeks and kissed her future husband, promising him with her kiss that she would always be his.

The End

∾

Check out Sarah Gay's second
Grant Brothers Romance

Nate Grant and Millie Moore's Story:
The Billionaire Patriot (excerpt below)

The Billionaire Patriot brings together TWO of Sarah Gay's family romance series: the Moores and the Grants

Moore Family Romances are set seven years before the Grant Brothers Romances begin

Max Moore's Story (Book 1):
The Gifted Groom

Miles Moore's Story (Book 2):
The Protective Patriot

Mason Moore's Story (Book 3):
The Patient Patriot

Millie Moore's Story (Book 4, six years later):
The Billionaire Patriot (excerpt below)

∼

Excerpt from The Billionaire Patriot:
Grant Brothers Romance, Book 2
and Moore Family Romance, Book 4

ive seconds, Nate Grant estimated as the football flew toward him in a perfect spin. *This is my moment!* His heart pumped with exhilaration as he sped down the field toward the end zone. Gray mist blanketed the opening of the stadium's dome. In response to the brewing storm overhead, the roof creaked as silver pie-sliced sections shifted to close and seal. Nate didn't allow his focus to veer from the incoming football, even as he knew the spectators in the stands tilted their faces to the roof of the world-renowned one-and-a-half-billion-dollar stadium.

Four. Six opposing defensive players neared him, their massive bodies occupying his entire peripheral vision. A confident smile split his lips; his opponents were close, but they wouldn't reach him before he caught the ball. He could taste victory, and there was nothin' in this world as sweet as making a touchdown in his team's home stadium in downtown Atlanta.

Three. Lightning pulsed across the darkening sky, blinding him as his fingers curled around the football. He instinctively pulled the ball into his chest, pivoted, and ran the last few yards to an end zone he couldn't see.

Two. Pop! A bolt of pain shot through his leg bones and into his pelvis as his opponent's shoulder hit his left knee. Still blind, he jumped, springing up and forward to clear the players who lunged for his legs. He braced himself as he fell, praying the ball had broken the plane—crossed the line of the end zone.

One. Nate smacked the ground to the sound of thunder cracking and echoing throughout the stadium. He held his breath during momentary silence before deafening applause and shouts marked another Georgia Patriots victory. He opened his eyes wide, but all he could see were white speckles. He blinked annoying stars from his eyes as he lifted the football and slammed it into the ground theatrically. Who said he couldn't enjoy his moment?

Zero. Agony hit him through the haze of adrenaline. He rolled onto his back, clutched the sides of his left knee, and rocked on his spine while he threw his head back and gritted his teeth. Then the real pain sliced open his chest—the emotional pain. His injury would bench him at least for the remaining season, if not forever.

In five seconds, he'd scored the touchdown of the season

for the Georgia Patriots, but in only one second, his lifelong dream to score a touchdown in the Super Bowl had been shattered.

~

*M*illie Moore yawned, then picked up her pace as she walked down the hospital corridor to the orthopedic surgical unit.

"Energy begets energy," Professor Santiago, her health sciences professor, had told her class while he jogged around the large auditorium, which caused his students to chuckle. That particular lecture remained clear in her mind; she thought of it every time she felt the least bit sluggish, basically from the day she'd started college until she'd finished her physical therapy degree. That class had also led her and her identical twin sister, Mazy, to choose careers in medicine.

She felt herself smiling as she waved her badge in front of the large double door keypad, remembering how Professor Santiago had smiled at each one of his students to greet them as they walked into the auditorium. That was the kind of doctor she wanted to be: someone who cheered her patients up simply by walking into the room and smiling. She held her arms up at her sides as she entered the cold, sterile room with a team of doctors dressed head to toe in white. "Beautiful day to start healing, don't you think?"

Dr. Stevens, the close-to-retirement orthopedic surgeon, cocked an eyebrow, his face lifting in amusement. "He's already out, Dr. Moore. You can save your positive speech for when he wakes."

"Blast," she responded with a sigh. "Perhaps the next one."

"He's my last surgery today. Mazy will be signing his discharge papers this evening." Dr. Stevens glanced up at the clock on the wall. "And where *is* your sister? We're ready to begin."

As a new orthopedic surgery resident, Mazy was the lowest woman on the totem pole and worked whatever shifts the hospital needed her to, yet she never complained about the long, grueling hours. According to Dr. Stevens, Mazy's potential rivaled the best physicians he'd ever worked with, and her lively, yet humble spirit made working with her pleasant—which was why she was the resident he picked for his surgeries.

It sounded like another intense day for Mazy. *Who wouldn't want a sleep-deprived medical resident working on them?* Millie kept her complaints and sarcasm safely tucked away in her head, remaining stoic and professional. She didn't want to mess up a good thing. Doctor Stevens allowed her to observe his surgeries as a courtesy, and he could retract the offer at the snap of his fingers. Already, Millie had gleaned invaluable knowledge from observing surgeries on muscles that she later rehabilitated. By understanding the severity of an injury and the surgery to correct it, Millie had the rare opportunity to treat her patients with greater insight.

That said, she didn't observe Dr. Stevens's surgeries merely for medical purposes; it also allowed her to spend time with Mazy. Simply being in the same room as her identical twin recharged her, made her happy in an inexplicable way—not to mention it had turned out to be the *only* way she could spend any time with her sister during Mazy's residency. They'd chosen to specialize in orthopedics and physical therapy in order to have careers that blended. They planned to share an office together when Mazy completed her residency, with the idea that a sports injury patient could meet with his or her orthopedic surgeon and physical therapist on the same day and in the same office. And their association with the Georgia Patriots would keep them busy. They had both attended the Patriot Academy high school, where their older brother, Mason, was the principal, and their other brother, Miles, had been a star NFL player who'd helped them get to the Super Bowl two of the three years he'd played with them—plus the team owner, Bucky, thought of them as his own daughters.

Mazy hustled into the room with a broad smile. "Sorry to keep y'all waiting. I needed to finish up down the hall."

"Did you see that touchdown?" asked the physician's assistant as she arranged the knives on the metal tray.

Millie bit at her bottom lip. "What touchdown? Is this guy a receiver for the Patriots?"

They all looked over at Millie with their own unique "where have you been?" expressions.

She held her tongue. They'd think she was a nutcase if she told them she'd refused to watch a single Patriots game since Nate started playing for them. She stepped closer to the surgical table, tilted her head to the side, and stared at the patient's face, which was partially covered by his oxygen mask. "Nate Grant." She narrowed her eyes. "You said he's completely out?" she asked Dr. Stevens with a raised brow. "So he'd never know what hit him if I slapped him hard?"

Continue Reading Book 2, The Billionaire Patriot at sarahgay.com/the-billionaire-patriot

ABOUT THE AUTHOR

Raised in Milwaukee, Wisconsin and Atlanta, Georgia, Sarah currently calls the northern Utah mountains, and the southern Utah red rocks, home. She graduated in Human Development from Brigham Young University and spent several years working as a Human Resource Professional. Her human resource skills are now utilized managing a workforce of four young children. When Sarah's team is being trained off campus, she dedicates her time to writing inspirational stories.

She would love to hear from you and can be contacted at sarah@sarahgay.com. To register for new releases, promotions, and free recipes, sign up for her newsletter at http://www.sarahgay.com/register/.

Made in United States
Orlando, FL
21 July 2022

20026000R00104